Emma Dilemma and the Two Nannies

McClain
Dad
Annie
Emma
Lizzie + Ira
Tim
MOM

Emma Dilemma and the Two Nannies

by Patricia Hermes

Marshall Cavendish Children

Marshall Cavendish Corporation
99 White Plains Road
Tarrytown, NY 10591
www.marshallcavendish.us

Library of Congress Cataloging-in-Publication Data
Hermes, Patricia.
Emma Dilemma and the two nannies / by Patricia Hermes. -- 1st ed.
p. cm.
Summary: Emma and her siblings plot to keep their beloved nanny Annie from going on a three-week vacation and leaving them in the care of the totally uncool, animal-hating Mrs. Potts.
ISBN-13: 978-0-7614-5353-6
[1. Nannies--Fiction. 2. Brothers and sisters--Fiction.
3. Family life--Fiction.] I. Title.
PZ7.H4317Emt 2007
[Fic]--dc22
2006026563

The text of this book is set in Souvenir.
Book design by Vera Soki

Printed in China
First edition
10 9 8 7 6 5 4 3 2

For the real McClain, with love

Table of Contents

Chapter One

Annie's Going Away

"Annie!" Emma cried. "You can't go!"

"You can't!" Tim cried. "It's not fair!"

"It's dumb!" McClain said.

Annie was their new nanny. Emma loved her. Tim loved her. McClain loved her. Even the twin toddlers, Ira and Lizzie, loved her more than almost anyone. She was the first nanny that any of them even liked.

The five kids were in the playroom at the back of the house, and Annie had just told them she was going away.

"Oh, me dears," Annie said. "Don't fret now. I won't be gone long. Just a little while."

"How little?" Emma asked.

"A few weeks."

"*Weeks*?" Emma said. She was so upset that

she squeezed her pet ferret, who was curled up in her arms. He squirmed and scrabbled his way up to Emma's shoulder.

"Sorry, Marmaduke," Emma whispered. And then she said, "Annie, you can't go! Why are you going? What about soccer? My away games? You were going to help me."

"I checked your schedule with your mum," Annie said, smiling. "You have no away games those weeks."

"You already told Mom and Daddy?" Emma exclaimed.

Annie nodded. "Just last night. They thought it was a good idea that I take a bit of a break."

"They did?" Emma said. She turned to her brother Tim. Tim was only ten and a half months older than Emma, and he was her best friend. And he was a worrier. Now, Emma thought, his eyes looked shiny.

Emma moved closer to him. "Here," she said softly. She held Marmaduke out toward him. Marmaduke was long and skinny and silver-colored and the most friendly, cuddly ferret ever. He slithered into Tim's arms and crawled up to his shoulder. Tim held him close. Woof, their enormous dog, came to stand beside Emma. Woof always knew when Emma was worried. He leaned his fluffy head against her leg.

McClain leaned against Emma's other leg, and Emma put her arm around her. McClain was the middle sister. She was always having mad fits. Mom said it was just the terrible twos. But McClain was almost five. Emma could see that McClain was setting up for a big fit now. She had stuck her bottom lip so far out that it looked as if she had a saucer tucked inside it.

All of them glared at Annie. Even the twins, Ira and Lizzie, stopped playing king and queen in the corner and stared. They were almost two years old, but they were super smart. And funny. They also talked as if they were four or something.

"Oh, me dears," Annie said. "You're all so upset with me! Don't be sad. You'll do just fantastic without me."

Fantastic? With Annie gone? Miserable is more like it, Emma thought.

"Now, come here, me dears," Annie said. She sat down on the couch and held out her arms. "Come on, all of you. Let me tell you about it."

Right away, Woof galloped away from Emma. He leaped onto the couch next to Annie. Lizzie got up and stumbled toward Annie, too.

"Wait for me!" Ira said.

They were both wearing the king and queen robes that Annie had made for them out of old bathrobes. Their robes were kind of long, though, and got twisted around their chubby legs. Annie helped them up to the couch. When they were settled in her lap, she looked at Emma and Tim and McClain.

"Come on, you guys," she said.

Emma didn't move. Tim didn't, either. Neither did McClain. They stood very close together.

"No?" Annie said.

Nobody budged.

"Don't you want to know where I'm going?" Annie asked.

Emma shook her head. Nobody answered.

"I'm going home to Ireland," said Annie. "To see me family."

"Then how come it's taking three weeks?" Tim asked. "Daddy flies to Ireland and back in five days."

Daddy was a pilot who often flew to Ireland and England and back. Tim missed him a lot when he was gone. Emma missed him, too. She knew Mom missed him a lot also.

"That's right," Emma said. "So how come?"

"Because I'm missing me sisters," said Annie. "I'll see them and . . . and then I'll come back to you."

Still nobody spoke. Emma knew that every single one of them was either mad or trying not to cry. Or both.

"It's just three weeks," Annie said softly. "Count the days. We'll make a paper chain, and you can tear off a link for each day . . ."

"Who will take care of us?" McClain said.

"While I'm gone?" Annie said.

McClain nodded.

"Well, your mum and dad, of course," Annie said. "But for nanny time? Not to worry. I have lots of nanny friends. I told your mum I thought I could find someone wonderful—so wonderful even she and your dad would be happy."

Uh oh. Emma looked at Tim. Tim looked at Emma. No! No new nanny. Not for three weeks. Whenever they got a new nanny, even for a few days, Mom and Daddy decided that the new one was the best one ever, and so they fired the old one. Of course, usually, after a while, they fired the new one, too. They'd done it about a hundred times already. So what if they liked the new nanny better than Annie?

Annie was their friend—their best friend. She loved them and loved their pets and kept their secrets and played with them like she was just another kid, only a grown-up one, a young grown-up one. She came from Ireland and talked funny and dressed wildly and got into trouble sometimes along with the kids, and . . . and they loved her! Even Mom and Daddy seemed happy with her. Well, most of the time they were happy with her.

Even worse, why had Mom and Daddy said that maybe Annie needed a bit of a break?

"We don't need a nanny," Emma said quietly. "Not for just three weeks."

"Do, too," McClain said. "We're a handful."

Emma made a face. McClain liked to repeat stuff she'd heard Mom say.

"She'll be a bad nanny," McClain said. "I hate bad nannies!"

"Bad nanny," Lizzie echoed. She snuggled closer to Annie. Ira didn't say anything. He just had a worried look on his face.

"Now listen, me dears," Annie said. "You know Ireland is me home. When I come back, I might even bring me sister Mary with me for a visit. You know she's on the national soccer team. She could maybe coach you some. Now, wouldn't that be grand? And I'll bring you all presents."

"A hamster!" McClain said, inching away from Emma toward Annie. "I want a hamster."

"There're hamsters here," Emma said. "You don't go all the way to Ireland for a hamster."

"Mom won't let me have one," McClain said. "But if Annie brought one from Ireland, I bet she'd let me. Or maybe a kitten."

"We'll work on that," Annie said, smiling at McClain.

Lizzie squirmed around and looked up. She put one pudgy hand on Annie's face. "I want Pretty Ponies," she said.

"I want a helmet," Ira said. "With a face mask."

Emma didn't say anything. She was too old for bribes, although she did think a soccer jersey from the Irish team would be cool.

She picked up a soccer ball that had rolled under the table. "I'm going outside to kick the ball around," she said. "Tim, come on."

"Okay," Tim said. He was still holding Marmaduke. "Where should I put him?" he asked.

"I'll take him," Annie said.

Tim dumped Marmaduke gently into Annie's arms. The ferret twisted around and tried to crawl inside Annie's shirt. Woof sniffed at him.

Woof was really good with Marmaduke unless Marmaduke started to run around. Then Woof thought it was a game and chased him.

Now Emma stood watching Annie cuddle Marmaduke. Most nannies hated ferrets. One had even tried to kill Marmaduke with a shovel because she thought he was a rat. But Annie loved Marmaduke.

And Woof.

And the kids.

"When are you going?" Emma asked.

"Not for a month yet," Annie said.

Emma turned and started out the door, Tim following. Well, that was good, anyway. A month was a long time. Anything could happen in four weeks.

Once outside, Emma turned to Tim. "Mom and Daddy think Annie *needs a break*? That scares me."

Tim nodded. "Me, too." He looked worried—very worried.

"Don't worry," Emma said. "We'll come up with a plan."

And she would. Though right then, she hadn't a single idea in her head.

Chapter Two

Emma Comes Up with a Plan

Emma and Tim talked and talked. They talked about zillions of things that would keep Annie at home with them, but nothing seemed right. Emma thought about pretending to be sick. Annie would never leave her if she were sick. But how long could she keep that up? It would mean missing soccer season.

What if Mom had to go away at the same time as Daddy? Then Annie would *have* to stay. But no, Mom and Daddy always worked out their schedules so that if one of them was gone, the other was home nights.

It had to be something big and important to keep Annie from going. But what?

Emma thought and thought. She could break her leg. Annie would never leave her if she had a broken leg. But even to Emma, that seemed a bit extreme.

And that's when Tim had an idea. What if they were super, super good? That way, maybe Annie wouldn't need a break. And if she did leave for a while, and they were extra, super good, Mom would see that they didn't need anyone new to come in. A lot of Mom's work with the museum was done from her home office. Surely she could manage for three weeks if the kids were really good.

This was Tim's idea. So he and Emma called a kids' meeting, and they all agreed to try to be extra good, even Ira and Lizzie. Of course, Emma thought, the twins probably didn't have a clue about what they were agreeing to. And knowing them, they probably couldn't be super good, even if they tried. Still, she and Tim could help take care of them, so they shouldn't be too much trouble.

For one whole week, they tried—they really, really did. But then came two super horrible days. It was the weekend, Annie's time off. On Saturday, Daddy took the twins with him to Home Depot. Emma offered to go along to help out. In front of the store, Daddy got a cart and hoisted Ira into the seat while Emma held Lizzie's hand.

All four of them went through the big, sliding doors—when suddenly, Lizzie pulled her hand out of Emma's. She took off running. She disappeared; here, and then gone. They looked for her everywhere, and Daddy was frantic. He asked store security to help, and they closed down all the doors while they searched for her. It took fifteen whole minutes, and the police got called, and the loudspeaker announced that a little girl was missing, and everything was nuts. Finally, they found her. She was sitting on top of a lawn tractor. Somewhere, she had found a hard hat, and it was plopped on her head. After Daddy hugged her and scolded her and hugged her some more, he had to fill out all sorts of papers with the police and the store people and everything. Then when it was all over, Daddy told them they were going home. He said he didn't need that electric drill that much, anyway.

That's when Ira did something really awful. They were on their way out of the store, Daddy holding tight to Lizzie's hand, Ira riding in the cart, just as a man came walking in. He was kind of a fat man, and Ira reached out from the cart and poked him in the middle of his tummy. The man just laughed, but Daddy was really upset and apologized all over the place. Daddy got even more upset when Emma laughed. She couldn't help it. She had always wanted to do that when she was little.

Then on Sunday, Daddy discovered that Marmaduke had chewed all the buttons off his pilot uniform, and he was supposed to fly out in a few days—Daddy, that is, not Marmaduke. Next, the doorbell got stuck and wouldn't stop ringing, and Woof got so excited that he dribbled pee in the front hall, and Mom slipped in it. McClain fell off the swing and bit her tongue, and there was blood all over the place. She wasn't really hurt, but she cried so long and so hard that she finally cried herself to sleep and slept all afternoon. When nighttime came, she was wide awake and had to sit up in Mom and Daddy's bed and watch TV until she got sleepy. Daddy said he couldn't wait till Monday when Annie or *somebody* could help.

Emma thought maybe he meant he couldn't wait to fly his plane away from all of them. She also didn't like the way he had said *somebody*, as if any old nanny would do. Why hadn't he just said plain *Annie*?

One good thing was that on the weekend, Emma hadn't done anything wrong. Well, maybe one little thing, but it wasn't that bad, and besides, nobody knew about it yet. Probably nobody would even care about a tiny broken garage window.

Still, in bed that night, Emma couldn't sleep. She shut her eyes. She opened her eyes. She shut her eyes. She opened them *again*. She stared up at the ceiling. A car passed by outside, and the lights ran up the wall, across the ceiling, then down again. The room got dark again.

If only she could talk Annie out of going. She'd miss Annie so much, and she couldn't bear having another nanny. She remembered some of the bad nannies they had had—the one who made the kids take at least one bite of everything on their plates, things like brussels sprouts and kale, and every single lunchtime, at least one of the kids threw up. There was the nanny who bundled them in hats and coats and mittens and scarves when it was just September, and every one of the kids broke out in heat rash, and Emma felt like she was melting. There was the really bad nanny who wouldn't let them watch TV because she said TV wasn't good for them. She also wouldn't let them have anything with sugar in it—sugar cereals or cookies or anything. Mom kind of liked that nanny, but McClain had such a hissy fit about no TV, Mom finally told the nanny they could watch a little each day. That nanny quit right on the spot. And then there was the nanny who used duct tape to keep the twins from climbing out of their high chairs. Actually, that had been Emma's idea, but when Mom found out, she was so mad that smoke practically came out of her ears, and there went that nanny. And, of course, there were all the nannies who didn't like Woof and hated Marmaduke.

Now Emma thought of calling Annie on the phone, but she knew she shouldn't. Annie lived in her own apartment up on the third floor. She had her own stairway, too, in the back hall. And she had her own telephone. Once she was finished for the day, the kids were not allowed to go up to her apartment, and they weren't supposed to call her on the phone, either. Mom and Daddy said Annie needed some time to herself, without the kids.

Emma didn't believe that. But she didn't think this was the time to disobey, either. Not after this past weekend.

Emma sighed, turned over, and snuggled into

her pillow. She thought about getting Marmaduke out of his cage and bringing him to bed, but decided not to. Sometimes Marmaduke was just too wiggly for snuggling.

Annie had told her once that counting sheep was a good way to get to sleep. Emma decided to give it a try. She turned over. She lay flat on her back, her arms straight at her sides. She scrunched her eyes closed. She started with a row of fat, white sheep. She had them walk toward a fence so they could jump over it, one after another, after another. They got to the fence. They bumped into one another. They got all tangled up. They fell down. Not one of them went over the fence.

That was weird. Shouldn't imaginary things do what you wanted them to? Emma stood them up. She untangled them. She made them walk toward the fence again. This time, they tried to jump over the fence backward. They tumbled in a heap again. One of them scooted under the fence. They were running wild all over Emma's imagination. It was not restful.

Emma sat up. The silly sheep had actually given her an idea. She knew just what to do. She turned on her light. She went to her desk to look for paper and pencil. Her desk was kind of messy. Actually, it was very messy, not at all like Tim's. Everything in Tim's room was perfect. He even sharpened all of his pencils every night and laid out his clothes for the next morning. Emma wondered sometimes if she and Tim were actually related.

Now, she dug through the mess, found some paper that didn't have too much writing on it, and a pencil. It was just a little stub, but it would do. She would invite Annie to her room early in the morning. They could have a private talk. Emma would ask Tim to join in. Together, the two of them would talk some sense into Annie. Emma would leave the note in Annie's mailbox so she'd find it first thing in the morning.

On the outside of the door to Annie's stairway in the back hall, Annie had put up things she called mailboxes, though they were actually more like mail bags. They were made of soft, fuzzy stuff in the shape of sheep, almost like stuffed animals, but without the stuffing. That's because Annie said they reminded her of home—there were lots of sheep in Ireland.

The top one was for Tim because he was the oldest. The next was for Emma. Underneath was one for McClain, down low so she could reach it. And at the very bottom, two mail bags for Lizzie and Ira hung side by side. In the bags, the kids left things they wanted to give or show Annie—pictures they had colored for her, or handprints they had made at preschool. The little kids' mailboxes were always overflowing. Emma put in stuff for Annie, too, notes and her good papers from school, and sometimes little presents, like flowers.

Emma sat down to write the note.

Dear Annie, I need to talk to you tomorow morning. I meen, today. Today, I meen, when you read this. I'm writing this on Sunday. When you read this, it will be Monday. That is when I need you.

Pleaze come to my room if I am not awake. And wake me up. She looked at the note. She chewed on her lip.

She added, *It's about you going away. And that new nanny. Truble.*

She looked at it again. What else?

She thought for another minute. She stared at the note.

She added, *Counting sheep does not help. My sheep are out of contrul.*

Emma folded the note, slid her feet into her frog slippers, and peeked out her bedroom door. The house was quiet; all the lights were out but the night-light in the hall. The upstairs hall was long, and the door to Annie's stairway was at the end. Woof lay stretched out right across the middle of the hall. When they first got Woof, Daddy said he'd be a great watchdog. It turned out he was wrong; Woof was mostly a good playing-with dog.

"Okay, Woof," Emma whispered, as she tiptoed toward him. "I'm going to step over you. Don't jump up and trip me, okay?"

Woof raised his head. He blinked. He put his head back down. But as she started stepping over him, he scrambled to his feet. She had to grab at the wall to keep from falling.

"Woof, stop it!" she whispered to him.

She padded carefully down the hall, keeping away from the squeaky boards. Their house was very old, so parts of it were very creaky. Woof padded after her. Together, they crept to Annie's door. The glow-in-the-dark clock on the wall gave off barely enough light to see by. It was a little past midnight. Emma put her note in Annie's mail bag. She stood for a minute, looking at the door. Should she knock? No. She shouldn't. But she could listen. Maybe Annie was still awake? If she was, maybe she'd like to talk to Emma. Annie was lonely for her family in Ireland, Emma knew.

Very quietly, Emma opened the door. A crack. She could hear Annie's TV going softly. "Annie?" she whispered. She didn't really mean for Annie to hear her. She just kind of wanted to say Annie's name.

She listened some more. Woof pushed up against her leg. She reached down and pulled him closer. His ears went up. They both listened.

"Annie?" Emma whispered again, a tiny bit louder. Just to say her name.

The TV clicked off. It got quiet upstairs. Was Annie going to sleep?

Emma listened.

"Emma? Is that you?" It was Annie.

"It's me," Emma whispered back. "And Woof."

"Is something wrong? Do you want to come up?"

Emma opened the door wider. Woof burst through the door and scampered up the stairs, Emma right behind. "I do!" she said.

Annie was sitting on her sofa, and she opened her arms wide. Emma ran into them. Now everything was going to be all right. It would be all, all right.

Chapter Three

Mrs. Potts Arrives

Except it wasn't. Emma was so happy and relieved to be talking to Annie—or maybe she was so plain tired—that after a little bit, she fell asleep on Annie's sofa. Annie fell asleep right beside her. Woof fell asleep, too, all three of them lumped together in a heap.

When Daddy got up to take Woof for his early morning walk, there was no Woof to be found. That's when Daddy started calling Woof's name, and Woof went bounding down Annie's stairs, and then Mom and Daddy found out where he and Emma had been. Now Emma was in trouble, and Annie, too.

And then more trouble. At breakfast, Annie said a new nanny was coming to visit that afternoon, someone who might help out while she was gone. Annie put her arm around Emma's shoulders when she said that. The night before, sitting upstairs on her sofa, she had told Emma that of course she loved them. Of course she wasn't tired of them. Of course they were the best kids in the whole wide world. They weren't a handful at all!

But she did still plan to go to Ireland.

And now today, she was bringing in a new nanny.

"Today?" Emma asked. "A new nanny *today*?"

"Yes," Annie said. "And you wait and see. She'll be just grand."

Emma's heart fell right into her shoes. And that was the start of what Emma knew was going to be a very rotten day.

And it sure was. At school, she couldn't pay attention because of worrying about the new nanny. Mrs. Adams, her teacher, who was usually nice, wasn't nice at all. She scolded Emma for daydreaming. Emma got in a fight with her best friend, Luisa. When Emma had told Luisa that Annie was going away, Luisa said, "That stinks. Is she coming back?"

Emma had said, mad like, "Well, *duh!* Of course she's coming back!"

She knew she had been mean. The thought of Annie going away was just so scary, it made her say it that way. But then Luisa got mad at Emma for being so mean.

Finally Katie, who Emma really, really, really didn't like, got elected class president.

The only good thing that happened was that when it was time to go home, Tim's usual Monday music lesson was canceled, so he could ride home on the bus with Emma. At least he'd be there when they met the new nanny.

They got off the bus and walked slowly up the path together. Neither of them spoke. All of Emma's insides felt worried. It was like the time she got called to the principal's office for fighting on the playground.

As they went up the steps, Tim said, "If we don't like her, Annie will get someone else."

"Right," Emma answered. "And then Mom might hire the somebody else. Or else, maybe Mom's looking for somebody else, too."

Tim looked at Emma. "Is she really?"

Emma shrugged. She pulled open the door. "Come on. Let's go see."

The minute they got inside, Annie called, "Emma? Tim? Is that you? Come here and meet my friend. We're in the playroom."

Emma looked at Tim. He looked back. They both dropped their backpacks and walked slowly down the hall.

"Hi, Emma, hi, Tim!" Annie said as soon as they came into the playroom. "We're making masks."

Annie was sitting at the craft table. McClain was on her lap. Lizzie was on one side of her, and Ira was on the other. All of the kids were covered with clay from their legs to the tops of their arms and they *even* had some on their faces. Lizzie, especially, was a mess. Annie, too, had a streak of something blue on her face.

A fat little woman with round, owl-like glasses was standing beside Lizzie. She was trying to wipe Lizzie's face with a washcloth. Lizzie was having none of it, though. She kept turning her head this way and that, trying to get away.

"Her name is Miss Spots!" Ira said.

"*Mrs. Potts*," the nanny said over her shoulder.

Emma looked Mrs. Potts over. Behind her round glasses was a round face. Her short gray hair was cut in a circle around her face. She was wearing purple sweatpants and a purple sweatshirt. She looked a little like a fat eggplant.

Mrs. Potts dropped the washcloth and straightened up. She wiped her hands on her pants. "How do you do, Emma?" she said. She held out her hand.

Emma took it. Mrs. Potts's hand felt dry, like paper.

"I'm fine, thank you," Emma said, even though that was a big, fat lie.

"How do you do, Tim?" Mrs. Potts said, holding her hand out to Tim.

"I'm fine, thank you," Tim said. "I hope you are, too."

"You have lovely manners, my dears," Mrs. Potts said. "I think we'll get along fine." And then she turned back to Lizzie.

"*Miss Spots* is a funny name," Ira said again.

"Mrs. *Potts*," Mrs. Potts said again. She picked up the washcloth. "Now, Elizabeth," she said. "Just turn your face this way, and we'll get it over with. Here we go."

"No!" Lizzie said. She buried her chin in her neck.

With both hands, Mrs. Potts turned Lizzie's face upward. But she was no match for Lizzie. Lizzie twisted her head around. She grabbed the washcloth in her teeth. She slid off the chair and ran to hide behind Annie, the washcloth hanging from her mouth.

Mrs. Potts looked at Annie. "Is she always like this?" she asked. She reached for Ira. "Can I clean you up now?" she asked.

Obediently, Ira held out his hands.

But then Mrs. Potts realized she had no washcloth.

Annie gently took it from Lizzie's mouth. She handed it to Mrs. Potts. Emma thought Annie was trying not to smile.

"Okay, here you go, little man," Mrs. Potts said as she went to work on Ira. "Not at all like your sister, are you?"

"I'm not yittle," Ira said.

"You're not *what*?"

"Yittle!" Ira said. "I'm not a yittle man."

"He means *little*," McClain said. It was the first thing she'd said since Emma came in. "Don't call him 'little,'" she said. "He doesn't like it."

"Well," Mrs. Potts said, "we'll have to work on pronouncing our *L* sounds now, won't we?"

She finished cleaning up Ira, then walked around to the back of Annie's chair and reached for Lizzie. "Shall we just get this over with?" she asked.

But Lizzie wasn't about to get it over with.

She scooted away, rounded the chair, then buried her face in Annie's lap. McClain put her hand on Lizzie's hair, as if she were protecting her.

"Tell you what, gang," Annie said, straightening up and gently removing the kids from her lap. "Let's go to the kitchen and get our snacks. Then we can tell Mrs. Potts all about our afternoon schedule." She turned to Emma and Tim. "You two will help Mrs. Potts learn our routine, won't you?"

Emma looked at Tim. They both nodded. Emma wondered how much of the routine she could get away with making up.

"In my day, children didn't have snacks," Mrs. Potts said as they went down the hall to the kitchen. "Three square meals a day was just fine for them."

Emma slid a look at Tim. He looked pale.

"Oh, my," Annie said, laughing. "Times have changed. My children love their snacks. Mallomars. We love Mallomars, don't we, children?"

When they were all settled at the kitchen table, Mrs. Potts looked around the room, shaking her head. "I've never seen such a big house," she said. "How many rooms do you have, anyway?"

Emma shrugged. She had no idea how many rooms were in their house. She had never counted. It was just a big, old house—really old.

"In my day, we didn't have such luxury. And we had just one bathroom," Mrs. Potts said.

Annie laughed. "We did, too. And just two bedrooms for me and me seven sisters. Oh, we had many laughs, we did. Imagine eight girls in two bedrooms."

Emma felt kind of sad. Annie really did miss her family.

Annie went to get the cookies as Woof came galloping into the room. He padded from one to the other, sniffing each lap, looking to see if anyone had any cookies yet.

"No, no," Mrs. Potts said when Woof stuck his nose in her lap. She waved her hands and twisted away from him. "Go, go! Shoo!" She looked at Annie. "I'm not much for dogs," she said. "I told you that. Especially ones bigger than I am."

"How about ferrets?" Emma asked.

"Ferrets!" Mrs. Potts said. Her eyes opened wide. "They're those nasty-smelling creatures, right?"

"Marmaduke isn't nasty smelling," Emma

said. "He's very sweet."

"He doesn't smell at all because Emma doesn't wash him much," Tim said. That was true, too. If you washed a ferret too often, it did something to its fur and made it smell.

"He doesn't bite," McClain said. "He just nibbles."

"You mean you have a ferret in this house?" Mrs. Potts said. Again, she looked at Annie. "You didn't tell me that."

Annie laughed. "Not to worry. Marmaduke is a darling. Besides, he mostly stays in his cage." She smiled at Emma. "Doesn't he, Emma?"

Emma smiled back. Yes, *mostly*.

She looked at Tim. He grinned and gave her a thumbs-up under the table.

Emma grinned back. Because she suddenly felt better, a whole lot better. It wasn't only about Marmaduke, either. Something that Annie said had given her an idea, an idea that would fix this whole entire problem.

Chapter Four

Book Fair Trouble

Like Mrs. Potts said, their house was really big with lots of rooms. There was a children's bedroom that wasn't even used, because Ira and Lizzie liked sleeping together. There was a guest room on the first floor with two beds and a bathroom. And Annie had her own apartment with an extra bedroom on the third floor. That meant there was plenty of room for all seven sisters to come visit. For Annie, it would be just like being home, eight sisters all together. She would be so happy. And wouldn't she be surprised? Then, of course, she wouldn't have to leave the kids, and there would be no need for Mrs. Potts or anyone else. Even Tim thought it was a good idea.

They had to work fast, though. So that night

they wrote a letter and invited the sisters to come. They asked them to please come quickly. They warned them not to tell Annie. It would be a really, really big surprise. Emma knew the address and even had the right stamps because she and Tim and the kids often wrote to Annie's sisters. Just a few days ago, Emma and Tim had sent them their new school pictures.

Emma put the letter in the mailbox. She lifted the little flag so the mailperson would know a letter was ready to go out. She and Tim figured it would take about a week for the letter to get to Ireland, and another week for the sisters' letter to get back. All they had to do was wait. Just two weeks. She wished like anything that the sisters had e-mail. That would be a lot faster. But when Emma had asked about it once, Annie said e-mail meant computers, and computers meant money. The sisters didn't have much of that, Annie said.

When Emma left for school the next day, she didn't mind that Mrs. Potts would be there when she got home. Well, she didn't mind too much.

At school, the Book Fair had started, and Emma loved books. She had an envelope with money that Mom had given her. When it was her class's turn to go to the gym to choose books, Emma made sure she was in line next to Luisa. They had made up from their little fight the day before. Mrs. Adams had gone to the gym ahead of them and left bossy Katie to be in charge of the line.

Katie was good at everything. That's why she got to do important things like lead the line and be class president. She was tall and had sun-streaked, thick, shiny blonde hair and wide blue eyes. She was really pretty. Emma kind of wished she wasn't.

"What books are you getting?" Emma asked Luisa. They weren't supposed to be talking in the hall, but Emma spoke very quietly.

"Soccer books," Luisa said. "They never have good ones about girls' soccer, though. Only boys'."

"I know," Emma said. She and Luisa both loved soccer. Luisa was on the traveling soccer team, same as Emma. Katie was on the team, too. She played left wing, striker, just like Emma. But Katie was only second string, and Emma was first string. Katie was getting better, though. And that worried Emma.

"I want a ferret book, too," Emma said. "But they never have them, either. And you know what else?"

"What?" Luisa said.

"Remember how I told you Annie's going away?"

Luisa nodded. "Yes. But she's coming back."

"Right," Emma said. "But guess what? She may not go at all. Because I invited all her sisters to come visit here. It's going to be a surprise."

"Really?" Luisa said. "Annie doesn't know they're coming?"

"Nope," Emma said.

"Way cool," Luisa said. "Was that your mom's idea?"

Emma looked at her feet. She shrugged, then shook her head no. Though, really, she didn't think Mom would mind. Much.

"It must be fun to have a bunch of sisters," Luisa said. She sounded a little bit sad. Luisa didn't have any sisters, or brothers, for that matter.

"Yeah," Emma said. She thought of her own sisters and brothers. "It is nice. Mostly."

"You're not supposed to talk in the hall," Katie said, turning around from the head of the line and glaring at Emma.

"Then why are *you* talking?" Emma said.

Luisa giggled. So did some other kids.

Katie made a face before turning back. Emma thought that some day Katie would make a really good teacher.

When they got to the gym, they had to wait in the hall until the fourth grade had filed out. Emma saw Tim with a whole pile of books.

He smiled at Emma. "Look!" he said. "Computers and wizards." He held up a book. "And I got this book on fairies for Annie."

"No. Talking. In the hall!" Katie said again.

Tim looked at Katie. He seemed startled. He turned back to Emma. "Bye, Emma," he whispered as his class moved away.

"Bye, Tim," Emma answered. She said it louder than was absolutely necessary. She turned and made a mean smile at Katie. For once, though, Katie didn't seem to notice or care. She was on tiptoe, trying to see into the gym.

Once the class was allowed inside, things got a little wild. Mrs. Adams had told them that they were to walk slowly up and down the aisles. But there was so much to see that it was hard not to speed up.

Luisa had already scurried over to the sports section, and Emma followed her. "Any soccer ones?" she asked.

"Nope!" Luisa said. "As usual."

Emma shrugged. "I'm going to look around,"

she said. She was just turning away when Katie swooped in. She reached for a book on the bottom shelf. She moved so fast, she almost knocked Emma over.

"Hey!" Emma said. "Watch out!"

"My coach told me about this book!" said Katie, yanking it from the shelf. "He told me to look for it. It's the best soccer book *ever*."

"What's it called?" Emma asked. She hadn't even noticed it. And then she saw why. The cover was all black—black, black, black. There was just a tiny soccer ball right down at the bottom of the cover, so it looked like it was rolling off the page. Well, who would pick up a book with a black cover? But it did have a cool title: *Soccer Tricks and Secrets That Even the Pros Don't Know.*

"I didn't see that," Luisa said. "Are there more?"

"Nope," Katie said.

"Can I see?" Emma asked. She held out her hand. "Just for a minute?"

"Sorry," Katie said. She didn't sound a bit sorry. "It's mine. I can't wait to show my soccer coach."

"*Your* soccer coach?" Luisa said. "Mr. George is all of our coach."

"I don't mean *team* coach," Katie said. "My

dad got me a personal trainer." And she flounced off with her book tucked under her arm, her blonde ponytail swinging behind her.

Luisa shrugged. "Big deal," she said. "I'm going to look for princess books."

Emma nodded. When Luisa left, Emma searched through the shelves for another copy of the soccer book. But no luck. She stood, thinking. What if it really did tell secrets that no one else knew? That could make Katie really, really good, better than Emma. And they played the same position. Annie had been helping Emma with her footwork. Maybe Annie would work some with Emma today? But again she remembered Mrs. Potts. Annie was busy yesterday, trying to teach Mrs. Potts all the things she'd have to know while Annie was gone. And she'd probably be busy today, too.

Emma sighed. But hopefully, in a few weeks, instead of Annie leaving, the sisters would be arriving. And then Emma wouldn't have to think about Mrs. Potts at all.

Emma chose a bunch of diary kinds of books, and a book about lizards and toads, and *The Secret Garden*. She loved that book. She put it in her pile and lined up with the rest of the kids to pay. Then they all returned to Mrs. Adams's room.

By the end of the day, Emma had mostly forgotten about the soccer book. Instead, she was worrying about Mrs. Potts again. She was especially worried about something Mom had said two times at dinner last night, something that Emma had almost forgotten—how responsible Mrs. Potts seemed to be. That's all that Mom and Daddy cared about. And Emma knew that sometimes they didn't think Annie was exactly responsible. There was that one time that Annie almost fell out of the tree, and then the time when she accidentally burned her passport in the oven—well, that was kind of Emma's fault, too. But Annie tried to do the right thing. Emma prayed like anything that the sisters would answer her letter soon.

When it was time to get on the bus, Emma ended up last in line. Right in front of her was Jordan, and right in front of him was Katie. Just as they got to the top of the steps, Jordan stepped on Katie's heel. Her shoe came off.

"Flat tire!" he yelled.

Katie swung around to face him. She tripped over her shoe. She fell into Jordan. He fell into Emma. All three of them tumbled backward down the steps of the bus.

Katie yelled at Jordan, "You did that on purpose!"

Jordan said a bad word.

Emma didn't say anything. She was pretty surprised at what Jordan had said. The bus-line lady came running over.

Emma picked herself up. She wasn't hurt, and Jordan didn't look hurt. But Katie's lip was bleeding. And everybody's backpacks had fallen open. Book Fair books were spilled all over the place, though Jordan still had one book in his hand.

The bus-line lady took both Jordan and Katie over to the side while Emma bent to pick up the books. She hated to see books all mashed up! She separated them carefully into piles. Her books. Katie's books—all the ones with the medals on the cover—and war and science fiction books that had to be Jordan's.

And there, underneath the books and mess of papers, on the very bottom of the pile, was the soccer book with the black cover. The soccer book with all the secrets.

Emma looked around.

The bus driver was sitting behind the wheel, staring straight ahead, bopping his head around to some tune playing inside his head. The kids on the bus were laughing and poking one another. Some were staring out the windows at the bus-line lady wiping blood off Katie's chin. Jordan was standing off to the side, reading a book while he waited to be yelled at.

Quickly, Emma slid the soccer book into her pile. Just for tonight. She would read it to see if there were any really good secrets, then return it to Katie tomorrow. She'd just tell her that in the mess, it got mixed up with her books. That was pretty much the truth, too.

She stuck the rest of Katie's books into her backpack and snapped it shut tight. She even fastened the buckle part that everyone usually lets dangle. And she put her own books—and the soccer book—into her own backpack. Her heart beat a little faster when she did that. But she was only borrowing it.

And then she thought of what Annie would say. Annie always told the truth, even when it got her in trouble. She wouldn't even lie about little stuff to Mom and Daddy. Emma sighed. She wished she could be as good as Annie. But just for a moment, she was glad that she wasn't.

Chapter Five

Marmaduke Makes a Mess

When Emma went to bed that night, she felt better than she had in a while. First, she had the book of soccer secrets to read and study. Second, late that afternoon, something wonderful had happened. At snack time, Emma had brought Marmaduke down to the kitchen, holding him on her lap while they all sat around the table having their Mallomars. Marmaduke had scrambled from her lap to Tim's, to Ira's, to McClain's, then to Lizzie's, begging for cookie crumbs. When he headed for Mrs. Potts, she made huffy sounds and waved her hands. She looked like she was trying to fly. She pushed herself away from the table.

"No, no, no you don't!" she cried. She

looked at Emma. "Get him away from me. Get him now."

Emma got up, went around the table, and scooped Marmaduke into her arms.

"Oh, me word," Annie said, shaking her head at Mrs. Potts. "Such a fuss. He's just a wee ferret!"

That made Emma smile. It seemed to Emma that Annie didn't have much patience for Mrs. Potts just then. And that was a very good thing.

Now she brought Marmaduke into bed to snuggle with. She propped up her pillows the way she liked them for reading, then opened the book of soccer secrets. There were lots of diagrams in the book. Emma was pretty good at knowing how to look at a soccer field to see where team members and defenders were, and these diagrams gave some cool suggestions. Still, Emma didn't find much that she didn't already know.

She was only halfway through the book when there was a knock on her door. She slid the soccer book under the covers as Mom came in.

"Emma," Mom said. "Lights out, sweetie." She came in and pulled up the covers around Emma's shoulders. "Did you get some good books today?"

Emma nodded. "Lots of them," she said.

"Good. Sleep well," Mom said. She swept a hand over Emma's forehead and pushed back her hair to give her a kiss.

"Mom!" Emma said. She hated it when Mom did that. Her hair was still wet from her shower. If you pushed it back, it stood straight up in the morning. Mom always forgot that.

"Oops! Sorry," Mom said. She smoothed Emma's hair back down.

Emma looked at her clock. Eight o'clock was her bedtime, and it was just eight now. "Can I read just a little while longer?" she asked. "Please?" She put her hands together as if she were praying.

Mom smiled. "Okay, ten minutes," she said. "No longer, though. Promise?"

Emma smiled. "Promise," she said.

Mom got up, but when she reached the door, she turned and asked, "What do you think of Mrs. Potts?"

"She's stu— I mean, I don't like her much," Emma answered.

"Really?" Mom said. "She comes from the same agency as Annie. She has wonderful references. What don't you like about her?"

Emma shrugged. "Everything. She's no fun.

And she doesn't like Marmaduke."

"Well, I like her quite a bit," Mom said. "She's smart and very responsible."

Emma made a face. "So?" she said. "Annie's responsible!"

"But we need a substitute while Annie's on vacation," Mom said.

"I know!" Emma said. "Quit reminding me!"

Mom just smiled. "Good night, sweetie." She went out and closed the door. Emma made a face.

For a second, she worried that Mom hadn't said anything about Annie being responsible, too. But then she decided that didn't mean anything.

Emma went back to her book. She read those extra ten minutes. Then she turned out the light and settled down to sleep. But she worried. She really had to know everything in this book. Mom wouldn't mind if she read just a teeny bit longer, would she? She had to return the book tomorrow, and she just couldn't let Katie know more than *she* knew. She lit her tiny flashlight and took it under the covers with the book. She'd read for a few more minutes.

Marmaduke thought the flashlight was super cool. He nudged at it, trying to eat it. "Stop!"

Emma warned him. "Stop or I'll put you back in your cage."

Marmaduke snuffled. He gave up on trying to gnaw through the flashlight. He snuggled in close to Emma and in a minute was fast asleep. Emma didn't know how long she read, but she practically finished the entire book. She didn't find any really cool secrets, though. Most of the things she already knew, like how to head the soccer ball without causing serious brain damage. There were just a few things that were new to her, like the part about looking at one team member while sending the ball directly to another. She thought that was a cool thing to do, but it would take some practice. Finally, when she thought her *eyes* would roll right out of her head, she closed the book, turned off the flashlight, and fell asleep alongside Marmaduke.

She was really exhausted. It had been a hard day, but a good one, in the end. She dreamed that she kicked a winning goal, and her team won the World Cup Soccer championship. Annie's sisters wrote a letter congratulating her, and it arrived in little shreds, but she could read it, anyway. Then there was a big parade for her team, marching down the avenue in

New York City. People threw ticker tape down on their heads. So many teeny bits of paper! Emma had seen that happen when the New York Yankees won the World Series, and she thought it was pretty cool.

Emma dreamed and dreamed. But then, something felt weird to her. Something was tickling her. She woke up. She heard a sound. She looked around. Woof had nosed his way into her room and was settling beside her bed. She reached a hand out and patted him.

She turned over and went back to sleep.

But something weird was still happening. Something was tickling her face. She rubbed her nose. She turned over again. Her bedside clock said five fifty-five. Emma loved fives. She smiled to herself. That meant this was going to be her lucky day.

Something was still bothering her. What a real-feeling dream, all those bits of paper floating around. She sat up. She peered down at her bed. What was all that stuff? It really looked as if there were bits of paper all over her blankets. She leaned over and stared more closely. No, not paper. Feathers. There were feathers everywhere!

"Woof," she said softly. "Did you chew up a pillow again?"

Woof had done that before, shook and shook and shook a pillow till there was no stuffing left and feathers flew everywhere.

Woof looked up at her. He wagged his stubby tail.

"I hope you didn't. Mom will have a fit."

Woof smiled. Then he sneezed.

It must be feathers. What pillow, though?

Emma slid out of bed and turned on the light. The stuff was all over the place. All over her bed. All over the floor. All over her pillow. Lots and lots of teeny, weeny bits of—not feathers. Paper.

Paper!

"Marmaduke?" she said.

Where was Marmaduke? She looked in his cage. Empty. She remembered. She had fallen asleep with him in her arms.

She lifted the blankets and peered underneath. There he was, peeping up at her. She reached for him. "Marmaduke," she said, scooching him from his hiding place and into her arms. "What's this . . . ?" And then she knew. Just like that, she knew.

The book. The soccer book!

"Marmaduke!" She didn't yell. Her voice came out all squeaky. She dropped him onto the bed. He flattened himself as flat as a snake, the way he did when he knew he was in trouble.

"Marmaduke, you didn't!" she said.

She dove under the covers. No book. She threw the covers back. She rooted around on the bed. On the floor.

He did!

The book. The soccer book. It was on the floor beside the bed. What was left of it. She picked it up. Shredded-up paper. A mangled cover with teeth marks. She could hardly breathe. She could hardly think.

She turned around. Marmaduke. He was still on the bed in his flattened-out state. Emma snatched him up and carried him over to his cage. She plopped him inside, kind of hard.

"Bad Marmaduke!" she said. "Bad, bad—*smelly* ferret!"

She set the cover down hard. She piled the heavy books on top as extra security, in case he figured out how to open the lock, as he'd done before.

Marmaduke looked up at her worriedly.

And then she thought—maybe he only did this because he knew it was Katie's book. Maybe he smelled Katie on it, so he thought he should tear it up. But that was no excuse.

Still, she reached in and scratched his head. Then she sat on the side of the bed, her heart pounding hard. What was she going to do? It wasn't her own book! She shouldn't even have taken this book! She had stolen it! Katie would kill her. She'd tell everybody that Emma was a thief and . . . What a dilemma!

She looked at Woof. "What should I do, Woof?"

Woof didn't answer, but he pushed his head against her legs like he did when he knew she was worried. She just sat there, struggling not to cry.

Annie, she thought. Annie could help her. But that made the tears really push up to her eyes. Annie. She didn't dare go up to Annie's apartment again.

And even if Annie didn't go away, even if her sisters did come visit, she wasn't sure that Annie—or even her seven sisters—could help her out of this mess.

Chapter Six

Emma's Awful Secret

Annie couldn't help her. Because she wasn't there. Annie had taken Mom's car before breakfast to go across town to pick up Mrs. Potts. There was a bus strike or something, and Mrs. Potts didn't have a car. Mom was frantic because she had an important museum committee meeting. She kept checking her watch, waiting for Annie to come back. There was no way Emma could tell Mom about the book, especially when Mom was so hyper. Besides, Mom wasn't the best parent to talk to for this kind of thing. Daddy was better, but he was away.

Emma sat at breakfast with such a lump in her throat that she could hardly swallow. She wondered if she should pretend to be sick.

She kind of did have a stomachache, so it wouldn't take much acting. Still, what good would being sick do? Tomorrow, the book would still be missing.

There was only one thing she could think of—go to school and pretend that she knew nothing about the missing book. She knew this wouldn't be honest, but she couldn't admit that she had deliberately stolen it, either. She wished so much that Annie were here. And to make things worse, Emma wouldn't have time to talk to Annie alone after school, either, because Mrs. Potts would be around. She wished so much that Daddy was home. She wished so much that . . . that . . . she didn't know what she wished. She just wanted everything to be better.

After breakfast, Emma got her backpack and waited by the front door for the school bus to honk outside. She watched the little kids. Instead of being in the playroom as usual, they were in the front hall, waiting for Annie, happy as could be. They didn't even seem to worry that in a few weeks, Annie would be gone, maybe for good. Ira and Lizzie were swinging around and around the stair banister, trying to see who could get dizziest and fall down first.

McClain had all her dollies lined up on the stairs, seventeen or twenty-five of them, playing they were sick. She kept sending them to the doctor. The doctor was Woof.

Emma wished she could be a little kid again.

Even Tim wasn't much company right now. He had his nose buried in a wizard book. Besides, even if he hadn't been reading, she didn't feel right telling him what she had done. Tim was so honest. He was like Annie that way. He might just tell her to tell the truth.

When they got to school and had said the Pledge of Allegiance, the first thing on the schedule was a class meeting. Mrs. Adams had a class meeting every Wednesday. Each person was allowed to talk about class problems. There were all sorts of rules to follow in the meeting, but it was usually pretty cool. People could talk about what was bothering them, and other people could help solve the problem. Of course, the teacher always got the last word, but Mrs. Adams was pretty fair.

As they pulled their chairs into a circle, Emma kept sneaking looks at Katie. She thought maybe Katie hadn't even noticed her soccer book was missing. If she had, she'd have hollered about it by now, since she had a big mouth. Yet she hadn't said a word. Or was she just waiting so she could make a big show of it later?

When they were all settled, Mrs. Adams said she was pleased with how well they had been behaving. She congratulated them on their fine behavior on the new playground and reminded them each to work for the good citizenship awards that were given out each month. There were two awards. One was for best individual overall citizenship. And the second was an award for the student with the most improved behavior. Mrs. Adams looked at Jordan when she said that. Jordan was the worst-behaved kid in the class, but he had been acting less wild lately.

So far, every month, Katie had received the best citizen award. Emma wondered if she'd ever get that one. She doubted it. Maybe someday, though, she could get most improved.

Next Mrs. Adams had some suggestions about better behavior at the Book Fair, despite their having behaved pretty well. Then it was time for questions and problems.

Monica Jane was the first to raise her hand. She was a big fat pain. She always had a complaint. She said that kids kept picking on her. She was usually right, too. Kids did pick on Monica Jane. Emma felt a little sorry for her. She was kind of square looking, with a square face and eyes that popped out a little. She looked sort of like a frog. Worst of all, she burst into tears the minute anyone looked at her. That was one reason kids picked on her so much. If only she could stop being a crybaby. Today, she wanted to talk about how the boys were teasing her on the playground. Jordan had stolen her hat, and he and Greg played keep-away with it, she said. She added that it made her feel terrible.

Emma looked down at her lap. She thought it was funny. The boys did that to her, too, and all she did was grab her hat back. Not only that, but sometimes she stole their stuff first. It was just a game. She stole a look at Luisa. She could see that Luisa was trying hard not to smile.

Of course, Jordan raised his hand after that and said it wasn't true: he'd been trying really hard lately to get that good citizen award. Still, they all had to talk about how to work this out, and how to respect one another's property, blah, blah, blah. And then they got into the Big Talk about bullying. Bullying was the main topic in school these days, and Emma thought it was silly. If someone made fun of you, you got even, that was all. There were all sorts of ways to do that. And if someone punched you, you punched them back. Big deal.

Emma looked around the circle. Katie had been alarmingly quiet. It was so not like her to keep her mouth shut. She didn't even chime in about the bullying. Emma wondered if maybe Katie was sick.

Next it was Gordon. Gordon needed to talk about how much homework they got and how his mom said it was too much. Emma thought he was right.

The whole time Gordon was talking, though, Emma still kept sneaking looks at Katie. Could Katie not have noticed the book was missing? Maybe she forgot she'd even bought a soccer book? She was just sitting there, so still, watching Gordon like she was really interested in his problem.

After Gordon finished his presentation, Mrs. Adams said she'd think about cutting back on their homework. Wow! Emma could tell that Gordon had really prepared his talk. She thought that was pretty cool, deciding to go after something that way, planning it, then giving the little talk. And it seemed to have worked. Emma wondered if she could ever be as organized as that.

Next Mrs. Adams said that just one more person could speak. That's when Katie raised her hand.

"Yes, Katie?" Mrs. Adams said.

My soccer book disappeared. I had it yesterday, and now it's gone. The only person who could have taken it was Emma.

Those were the words that Emma expected. So she was completely shocked when Katie said, "Jordan stole my soccer book."

Emma just stared.

Mrs. Adams looked blank for a minute. Then she said, "Let's not use the word *stole*, shall we? Did he perhaps *borrow* it?" She turned to Jordan. "Did you, Jordan?"

Jordan wrinkled up his nose. "I don't know what she's talking about," he said.

"My soccer book," Katie said. "You asked to see it yesterday when we were standing in line for the bus. And I let you. But then you tripped me, and I fell down, and I got home, and the book wasn't there."

"Katie!" Mrs. Adams said. "I don't think this is the way to approach this problem. Why don't you just explain what happened? Slowly. From the start."

Katie took a big breath. "Okay," she said. "Yesterday we were waiting in line to get on the bus. Jordan asked if he could look at my soccer book. I said yes. He took it. Then we went up the steps of the bus. Jordan gave me a flat tire—I mean, you know, he stepped on the back of my shoe on purpose so my shoe came off, and kids call that a flat tire and . . ."

"Katie," Mrs. Adams said, holding up her hand. "Jordan had your book. Now, did he give it back to you?"

"No."

"I did too," Jordan said.

"Did not," Katie said.

"Jordan," Mrs. Adams said, turning to him. "Did you have the book?"

Jordan nodded. "I did! But I handed it back to her. I did, right before I . . . right before her shoe slipped off."

Mrs. Adams looked from one to the other.

"May I have my book back now, please?" Katie said. The words sounded nice enough, but Katie was mean looking. Her eyes were squinched up at Jordan.

Emma's heart went thumpity-thump. She hadn't ever thought this was going to happen. Katie didn't suspect her! She felt so relieved.

She felt so guilty.

Now Jordan was in trouble. His face was red. "I don't have your book!" he said. "I gave it back to you."

"You did not," Katie said. "You had it, and then you pushed and made us all fall down, and when I got home, the book wasn't in my backpack." Katie turned to Emma. "You saw the books. You picked them up. Did you see it? Was it there?"

Emma's heart was thudding crazily. She shrugged. "I . . . I don't remember," she said. "It could have been. I mean, I don't know. I don't remember."

"See?" Katie said. "She doesn't remember seeing it. Because you still had it. I saw you reading it when the bus-line lady was cleaning up my cut lip."

Emma remembered that, too. She had thought it was pretty funny that Jordan just stood there, waiting to be yelled at, and reading his book. But it wasn't the soccer book he was reading. She knew that for sure.

"That's not what I was reading!" Jordan said. "I was reading—"

Mrs. Adams held up her hand. "Maybe it's on the bus somewhere," she said. "I'll ask at the office. Meanwhile, let's all check our desks now. It's a good opportunity to clean them out, anyway. We'll take everything out of our desks, and who knows what we'll find?" She smiled at the kids. "I'll clean mine, too."

Everyone stood up, ready to push their chairs back to their desks. Just last week, Mrs. Adams had put old tennis balls on the bottoms of the chair legs so that the chairs didn't make any noise when they were moved. Emma thought that was a shame.

Mrs. Adams went to her desk, and the kids went to theirs. The only sound was the quiet, hushy sound of the chairs with the tennis balls.

When Emma got to her desk, she began pulling stuff out—old candy wrappers, barrettes, broken crayons, a lollipop stuck to a notepad. She didn't know how to feel. Well, maybe she did. She felt relieved. She felt scared.

She felt very, very guilty.

Chapter Seven

A Letter from Ireland

When Emma got home from shool with Tim that day, they sat together for a minute on the steps outside. Neither of them wanted to go inside and see Mrs. Potts. Besides, Emma felt very worried in her stomach about the soccer book and Jordan. It really wasn't his fault. And he really was trying to get that good citizenship award. She decided to talk to Tim about it.

"Tim?" she said. "Remember the time you lost Daddy's watch?"

Tim nodded. "I wasn't supposed to have it."

Emma nodded. "Uh huh. And remember that at first you didn't want to tell Daddy?"

"Yeah," Tim said. "But I did."

"I know," Emma said. "But what if you sort of lost something that didn't belong to you?

Not lost it, just maybe broke it?"

"I didn't break Daddy's watch."

"I know!" Emma said. "I didn't mean that."

For a minute, Tim didn't say anything. Then he asked, "Why? Did you break something?"

Emma took a deep breath. She looked down at her shoes. "No," she said. "But Marmaduke did."

"Oh," Tim said.

"And it wasn't mine," Emma said.

"Oh," Tim said again. "Can you fix it?"

Emma pictured the bits of chewed-up book, the tiny strips of paper everywhere. She sighed. "No. And you know what's worse?"

"What?"

Emma sucked in her breath. She was about to tell the truth—that somebody else was being blamed for it—but she couldn't. She just couldn't.

She stood up. "Oh, nothing," she said. "Let's go inside."

They picked up their backpacks and went in. The house was unusually quiet. The door to the playroom at the end of the hall was closed, but they could hear music coming from inside. It sounded like someone was singing quietly to guitar music—soft music, like a lullaby. Was Annie trying to lull the little ones to sleep? She hadn't been able to get them to nap at all lately. She said they were outgrowing their naps, and even if she put them in bed, they played the whole time. Then they were cranky as anything by dinnertime. Maybe Annie had come up with something new to try?

Emma looked at Tim. "Is that Annie singing?" she asked.

Tim shook his head. "Doesn't sound like it. And Annie doesn't have a guitar."

Emma nodded. Maybe it was a recording?

"Should we go see?" Tim said.

"Hold on a minute," Emma said. She picked up the mail stacked on the hall table. She didn't really expect an answer from Ireland, not so quickly, but you never knew. She flipped through the envelopes and circulars.

"Tim!" she said. She whirled around. Tim was right behind her, and she almost stepped on him. "Oops, sorry. Tim, look!"

"A letter?" he asked.

"A letter. From Ireland. For us—you and me!"

"Open it," he said. "Open it quick!"

They both dropped their backpacks. Emma fumbled with the letter.

"They couldn't have gotten our letter so fast!" Tim said.

"Maybe," Emma said. "Maybe they did."

She tore open the envelope.

Tim leaned over her shoulder.

"Dear Emma and Tim," Emma read out loud. "Thank you so much for sending along your new school pictures."

Emma looked at Tim. "Rats!" she said. "It's just a thank-you note."

"Wait!" Tim said. "Read the rest."

Emma looked again at the letter. She read out loud.

"You are such beautiful children! We do think you have grown since you sent the first pictures just a few months ago.

"Annie tells us wonderful stories about you all. We can't wait for her to visit! Maybe someday we will come see you! We want to meet all of you, and Marmaduke and Woof, too. We'll have to save up our money, though, because it costs a lot. But who knows? Maybe someday.

"It has been raining here for three days, but just this morning, the sun came out. We are very happy for that. Write to us soon.

"With love from,

"Mary and Meagan and Elizabeth and Maureen and Kathleen and Brigid and Teresa."

Tim looked at Emma. "They didn't get our letter yet."

"No. They didn't say thanks for inviting us or anything," Emma said. "But they said they'd like to come."

"But they said they'd have to save up," Tim said.

"It doesn't cost that much," Emma said.

Tim sighed. "Anyway, they'll get our letter and answer us soon. We only sent it three days ago." He sighed again. "Mail takes so long."

"Too long," Emma said. And then, suddenly, she had an idea. Annie called home a lot on her cell phone. Sometimes, she even let Emma and Tim and the little kids talk to her sisters. Why hadn't she thought of it before? "Tim!" she said. "Why don't we call them?"

"Call them?"

"Yes, call them. Annie's cell phone. Remember?" she said.

Tim frowned. "We could, I guess."

"Remember how she showed us?" Emma said. "She punched in the number seven for seven sisters. And it dialed right to them."

"How can we get her phone, though?" Tim asked. "We couldn't tell her or it wouldn't be a surprise. If only they had e-mail."

"Well, they do. But they have to go to a café or something for it," Emma said. "And they might not go right away. But I have an idea about the phone."

Tim just looked at her.

"You know how she's always losing her phone? She leaves it on the table or the couch and stuff. She can never find it."

"Yeah?" Tim said.

"So," Emma said, "next time we see it lying around, let's take it and run up to our room and call. And then we'll give it back to her. We'll tell her we found it, that's all."

Tim frowned.

"She won't know," Emma said. "And besides, it's not like it costs a billion dollars or anything. Remember how she told us she has this great deal for calls to Ireland?"

"I know," Tim said.

Just then, the door to the playroom opened, and Annie stuck her head out into the hall. "Hey, you guys!" she said softly. "You're home! Come on in here and see what's happening."

"What?" Emma asked.

Annie put a finger to her lips. "Come see," she said softly. She turned back to the playroom. "Come on."

Emma put the letter in the pocket of her jeans. She and Tim went down the hall. There was no music coming from the playroom anymore; no guitar, anyway. The whole house was really, really quiet. You could almost hear yourself breathe.

They peeked inside. There, stretched out on the big sofa, was Lizzie, sound asleep, her head resting on Woof. On the other end of the sofa was McClain, also sound asleep, her raggedy, favorite blanket against her face.

And between them was Mrs. Potts. She was humming softly, a sweet sound, a lullaby, maybe. And on her lap—on her *lap*!—was Ira, his thumb in his mouth, the stuffed rabbit he called Puppy clutched in his arm.

Emma turned to Annie, her eyes wide. Annie was smiling.

Emma turned back to Mrs. Potts.

Mrs. Potts smiled at her. And then, she winked!

Just then, Ira sighed and turned a little. He put his little hand up on Mrs. Potts's shoulder, winding it around her neck, the way he did sometimes with Annie. Emma stared at all three of the kids.

The little traitors.

Chapter Eight

One Crazy Cat

Another week went by. No letter arrived from the sisters. Daddy had flown to Ireland and back again. Mrs. Potts was still showing up every afternoon. And time was running out. In just one week—eight days, actually—Annie would be leaving. At school, Emma felt really, really worried about Jordan and the soccer book. Mrs. Adams had told the class that the book had just been lost and not to worry about it; these things happened. But she seemed a little annoyed at Jordan, like maybe she didn't believe him. And Katie was being really, really mean to him. Even though Emma didn't like Jordan very much, it made her feel awful. But maybe worst of all, Annie hadn't misplaced her phone all week.

Neither Emma nor Tim had had a single chance to snatch it up for that super important phone call to Ireland.

But there *was* some good news. When Daddy got home, he said he wouldn't be flying out again for a little while, and he'd be home for three whole weeks. It was a Friday, and he was sitting on the couch with the little ones crawling all over him and cuddling and talking nonstop. Tim was on the floor reading, leaning back against Daddy's legs. Mom had come home from a day in the city and was plopped down, her head resting against the back of her favorite recliner chair, her legs stretched straight out in front of her. She looked flat, like she'd been ironed. And Annie was getting ready to drive Mrs. Potts home.

"Kids," Annie said as she got out her coat. "I was thinking I'd stop at the pumpkin farm on the way back. Anyone want to come along?"

Perfect, Emma thought! Once Mrs. Potts was dropped off, Emma would finally have a chance to talk to Annie alone. And then she thought of something even better: Annie always took her cell phone in the car and sometimes forgot it there.

"I want to go!" Emma said.

"I want to, too!" Tim said, dropping his book and scrambling to his feet.

"Me, too!" Lizzie said.

"Me, three!" McClain said.

"Wait for me!" Ira said.

Annie smiled and went to get the car keys. All three little ones jumped off Daddy's lap and scrambled down from the couch.

"Oh, no!" Mrs. Potts said. She moved toward the little kids, turned them around, and herded them back to Daddy. "You must ask permission from your dad and mom now that they're home. Parents have the final word. Say, *Daddy, may I go? Mother, may I?*"

The little kids just stared at her. They seemed confused.

Mom released the lever on her chair and sat straight up. "How very clever of you, Mrs. Potts," she said. "You really have a wonderful sense of what to expect from children."

"In *my* households, the parents *always* have the last word," Mrs. Potts said.

My *households?* Emma thought. *Like Mrs. Potts owned them or something?*

Daddy just laughed. "It's okay if they go," he said. "I'm going to be home for three weeks now. You guys go and have fun."

"Yes, you may go," Mom said, waving a hand at all of them. "It will give me some time alone with Daddy. And maybe when you get home, we'll get pizza or something."

"Good," Mrs. Potts said. "The little ones all had nice long naps today, so they should be fine."

Mrs. Potts began helping the little ones into their sweaters and coats. She had to search for Ira's shoes. Ira took off his shoes every chance he got, and they were always getting lost. Annie didn't care at all if Ira went barefoot, but it drove Mrs. Potts crazy. Now Mom found one shoe under the couch, and Mrs. Potts found the other one in the block bin. Mrs. Potts wriggled them onto Ira's feet.

"You mustn't run around barefoot," Mrs. Potts said to him. "How many times have I told you? You can get a fungus infection that way."

"Fun and guts!" Ira said.

"Right. Fungus. And it's not nice at all," Mrs. Potts said.

Emma watched Mom watching Mrs. Potts. Mom had that special kind of look on her face that meant she really liked this new nanny. Emma was pretty sure that Mom was thinking Mrs. Potts was the most perfect nanny ever.

"It's not nice trying to scare little kids,"

Emma muttered, scowling at Mrs. Potts and then at Mom. But she said it super quietly. She knew Mom wouldn't like her to be fresh. She went and scooped Ira into her arms and hugged him close. "It's okay to be barefoot," she whispered to him.

"I know," he said back.

When Annie reappeared with the keys, they all left.

They drove across town, Mrs. Potts and Annie in the front seat, Emma and the other kids behind them in the van. Annie drove really, really slowly. In Ireland, people drive on the left side of the road, not like here, where you stay on the right. Annie once told the kids that when she first came to America, she'd driven a whole mile down the wrong side of the highway. Now, she was extra careful. She drove very slowly. Cars were always lined up behind her, honking.

Soon they turned into a small, curved street and pulled up in front of Mrs. Potts's little house. It was kind of curved in front, with a little turret on top. It reminded Emma of a little teapot. Statues were lined up along the walk— two wooden children, a boy with a frog in his hands, a girl with a puppy in her arms, and a stone dog with a flower basket in his mouth.

There was also a cat, a real cat, sitting on the front walk. It was a wispy gray cat with a bunch of fluffy fur around its face, almost like a lion's ruff. It was super skinny, and Emma could see that it was shivering.

"You have a cat!" McClain shouted.

Mrs. Potts shook her head. "Not mine. I hate cats. That's a stray. Been hanging around here for weeks. Nobody seems to own him."

"He's hungry!!" McClain said. "He's so skinny. Oh, Annie, can I get out and pet him?"

"No!" Mrs. Potts said. "No, don't pet him. Don't encourage him. That's why I don't feed him. He'll keep hanging around. I even put up signs asking who owns him and asking them to come get him. But nobody's claimed him, and he keeps begging. He comes to my door, and I just shoo him away."

"But you *have* to feed him!" McClain cried.

"Oh no I don't!" Mrs. Potts said. She got out of the car then. "Bye, kids," she said. "See you tomorrow!" She waved and started up the walk to her house.

"Bye, Miss Spots!" Ira and Lizzie yelled.

The cat looked at her but didn't follow. He just sat there, staring up at the car and meowing, like he knew McClain was already his new friend.

McClain took off her seat belt and tumbled over the seat into the front, where Mrs. Potts had been sitting. "Annie!" she said. "Don't go! Poor cat. He's hungry. Let's take him home. Please?"

Annie sighed. "I know," she said. "Poor little mite. He looks starved, doesn't he? But we can't take him home. You have a dog. And a ferret."

"So now we can have a cat!" McClain said.

"Your sweet mother doesn't even want you to have a hamster," Annie said.

They all looked out the window of the car. The cat sat on the sidewalk, looking up at them and meowing pitifully.

McClain's face bunched up the way it did when she was about to cry. Or have a mad fit.

"I have an idea," Emma said.

"We can bring him home?" McClain said.

"No," Emma said. "But we can take him to the vet, to our vet, Dr. Pete."

"Right!" Tim said. "Dr. Pete can feed him and give him a checkup. And he always has signs up for adopting pets on his bulletin board and—"

"And we can adopt him," McClain said.

"It costs money for the vet," Annie said.

"Oh," Emma said. "Mom won't mind that." She was pretty sure that was true. Mom wouldn't mind them taking him to the vet. Mom was very kindhearted with animals, even though she always pretended not to like them very much. But keeping the cat? Well . . . Mom would mind that. A lot.

"I like cats," Ira said.

"They don't scratch," Lizzie said.

"Sometimes they do," Ira said.

Annie just smiled. "Oh, me dears, I think I'm getting meself into trouble. But you're right. We can't just leave the poor darling here, now, can we?"

She unfastened her seat belt and opened the car door. All of the kids unsnapped their seat belts and spilled out of the car after her. They crouched down by the cat.

The cat rolled over, showing its belly. It began to bat its little paws in the air. "Oh, Kelley!" McClain said. "You are so cute!"

Kelley?

"You're my cat, right, Kelley?" McClain said.

"You said you wanted a hamster," Emma said.

"Or a cat," McClain said. "I really, really want a cat."

Suddenly, the cat lay very still. It didn't even appear to breathe.

McClain touched his belly. He still didn't move.

"What happened?" Emma asked. She looked at Annie.

"Is he dead?" Tim asked.

Nobody answered. Even the twins were still.

Emma held her breath.

Suddenly, the cat leaped up, ran around and around in circles, then lay down again. He rolled over and over.

"Crazy cat!" McClain laughed.

"You little trickster, you!" Annie said. "Shall we take you to the vet now?"

Emma looked at her watch. It was almost four o'clock. The way Annie drove, the vet would be closed by the time they got there.

"Annie?" Emma said. "Should we call Dr. Pete and tell him we're coming?"

"Oh, good idea," Annie said. "My cell phone is right there in me purse, I think. I'll wrap Kelley up in me sweater so he won't scratch. I don't think cats like car rides very much."

Emma scrambled back into the car. Tim got in after her. She got Annie's purse. She slid a look at Tim. He nodded.

The cell phone was there. She took it out and dialed Dr. Pete. She knew the number by heart because Dr. Pete cared for Marmaduke, too. She told him to wait because they were on their way. And then, instead of putting the phone back in Annie's purse, she pushed it down into the seat between her and Tim. She'd dig it out when they got back home.

As they settled into the car, McClain holding fast to Kelley all wrapped up in Annie's sweater, Emma thought about her day. She still had to deal with Marmaduke and the chewed-up book. She still had to deal with Katie and Jordan, who was in trouble because of her. And the biggest, the Annie-going-away problem. And now, there was this new kitten that McClain already loved and Mom was going to hate. She was very afraid that her whole world was suddenly getting away from her.

But she had the cell phone. She and Tim would call the seven sisters that very night.

Chapter Nine

Emma Takes Charge

Emma looked around the dinner table. Everyone seemed to be in a good mood. Daddy was always happy when he got back home after being away on a trip. He hated being away from his family for a long time. Mom had changed out of her business clothes, and she seemed relaxed and happy, too. She was smiling at Ira and Lizzie, even though they were clobbering each other with slices of pizza.

"That's enough, gang," she said as she separated them. They didn't even scream.

Tim was quietly happy. Even though Emma knew he must be worried about the hidden cell phone, she also knew that he was glad they would be making that phone call. The phone was safely hidden in his room. They hadn't had time before dinner to call, but afterward, they'd do it.

McClain, of course, was super happy. She maybe figured that Kelley was already hers. She was chattering away about preschool and dance lessons to Daddy.

And Kelley was at Dr. Pete's office getting a checkup. Dr. Pete promised not to say a word to Mom and Dad until the kids had had a chance to tell them that they were adopting a cat. Or, well, like Annie said—till they had a chance to *ask* if they could get a cat. Annie had gone upstairs to her own apartment now that her day with the kids was over. And Emma had been the one chosen to tell about the cat. Or ask. Even the little kids thought she'd do it best.

Now Emma sent a look to Tim, her eyebrows up. He nodded.

She waited till McClain was finished talking. Then she said, "Mom? Dad?"

They both looked at her.

"I have to tell you something," Emma said.

"What is it, toots?" Daddy said, smiling.

Emma took a deep breath.

"We got a cat!" McClain burst out before Emma could say a word.

"*What?*" Mom said.

"We did not!" Emma answered.

"Did too," McClain said. "You know it. Mom, can we keep her?"

"We did not *get* a cat," Emma said. "I mean, not exactly."

"We did too," McClain said. "We took her to Dr. Pete first, and then . . . "

Daddy put up a hand. "That's enough, McClain," he said. "Emma! What's this all about?"

Emma took another deep breath. "Okay," she said. "We found a cat today. When we took Mrs. Potts home. See, it was hanging around Mrs. Potts's house. It was starving, and Mrs. Potts wouldn't feed him."

"She wouldn't *feed* him?" Mom said.

"No! She said he wasn't hers," Emma said. "So Annie wrapped him up in her sweater and—"

"Wrapped him in her sweater?" Daddy said.

"Uh huh," Emma said. "Real tight. It was her good sweater, too, her red one."

Mom looked at Daddy. Daddy looked at Mom. They both shook their heads. Annie always said that you could never tell what anyone was thinking. Emma thought Annie was wrong about that. Right then, Mom and Dad were thinking bad things about Annie. And the cat.

"She had to," Emma said quickly. "Otherwise he could scratch. When we took him to the vet, I mean. In the car, I mean. 'Cause cats don't like cars."

"He played dead," Ira said.

"But he wasn't," Lizzie said.

"So we took him to Dr. Pete," Emma said. "And he gave him a checkup. And that's all."

"Wait a minute!" Mom said, holding up her hand suddenly. "Is there a cat in this house?" She looked around, as if she thought a cat was lurking somewhere nearby.

"No!" Emma said. "There's no cat here. He's at the vet's. At Dr. Pete's."

"It's a girl cat," McClain said. "She's pretty. And fluffy. Her name is Kelley."

Mom shook her head. She looked across the table at Daddy. "Honestly, sometimes I do *not* understand Annie," she said. "Imagine even *thinking* about bringing a cat into a household with a dog and a ferret. And five children. Why didn't she at least call us on her cell phone first? She is so irresponsible at times."

"Mo-om!" Emma said. "Annie *was* acting

responsibly. What were we supposed to do? Leave the cat to starve?"

Mom shrugged. "Nooo," she said slowly.

"Well," Emma said.

"And Mrs. Potts wouldn't feed him," Tim said.

Emma had a quick, brilliant thought. "And that was very *ir*responsible of Mrs. Potts!" she said. "Wasn't it?"

"Well, it wasn't very nice, that's for sure," Daddy said, frowning. "Who thought of taking the cat to the vet?"

Emma started to say, "I did." Because she had. But instead, she said, "Annie did."

"Well," Daddy said, "she used her head there. I'll talk to Dr. Pete in the morning, and we'll pay him for the care of the cat."

"Someone will adopt the cat," Mom said. "But not us. We are not getting a cat."

"We are too!" McClain said.

"We are not!" Mom said.

"We are too!" Lizzie said.

"We want a cat!" Ira said. He looked at Lizzie. "Or a hamster. Right, Lizzie?"

"No!" Lizzie said. "We want a cat!"

"We *are not* getting a cat," Mom said. "And that's all there is to it!"

McClain jumped down from her chair. She clenched both her hands into little fists. Her face got perfectly red. “We. Are. Getting. A. Cat!” she said. She stamped her feet and stormed out of the room. She stomped her way all the way up the stairs.

Emma knew just what McClain was going to do. She was going to lock herself in her room and slam things.

“McClain!” Mom called in a warning voice. “Don’t you slam things around up there.”

But McClain was already slamming.

“Mom?” Emma said. “Can we be excused? I have homework.” She jumped up from the table. She had just caught sight of Marmaduke. Somehow he had escaped from his cage again and was slinking across the hall toward the dining room. Woof hadn’t seen him yet.

Mom nodded. “Yes, honey. You kids go. Daddy and I will do the dishes tonight. But no more talk about the cat, okay?”

Emma crossed the room and scooped Marmaduke up into her arms. She buried her face in his fur. “Rascal,” she said. She hugged him. She had almost forgiven him for chewing up the book. But just thinking about that made her stomach feel a little jumpy again.

Mom looked at Marmaduke and made a face. "I see he got loose again. Imagine if there were a cat here, too. Now I don't want to hear one more word about a cat."

Emma glanced at Tim. She knew there would be plenty more words about a cat. But just then, she and Tim had a job to do. A phone call to make. To Ireland.

Chapter Ten

Emma Tells a Lie

Holding Marmaduke tightly, Emma raced up the stairs after Tim. It was noisy in Tim's room, though, with McClain slamming things around in the next room, so they took the cell phone down the hall to Emma's room. They could still hear her from there, but it wasn't as bad.

They closed the door, and Emma set Marmaduke down. Right away he scrambled up onto her bed, making a nest for himself out of all her pillows. Her book *The Secret Garden* was by her pillow, and she moved it to a safe place high on her shelf, next to her dolls.

"Okay," she said to Tim. "So what do we say? We tell them that we know Annie's supposed to go there soon, but . . . but she wants *them* to meet *us*! And so they have to come *here*, and she shouldn't go *there*. Right?"

"Right," Tim said. "But you're going to do the talking. Okay?"

"Okay," Emma said.

"And remember," said Tim, "we have to tell them it's a surprise so they don't say anything to Annie."

"Right," Emma said. "Because we don't want them to spoil the surprise."

"Emma?" Tim said then. "Do you think they'll really come?"

Emma sighed. "I don't know. They might. I mean, Annie's mom came here, and Annie came here. So why not Annie's sisters? It's not really that far. Daddy flies to Ireland and back every week or so. It's just like . . . like going to California or Florida or something. Right?"

Tim nodded. "I guess," he said. He punched the button for number seven. He listened for a moment, then handed the phone to Emma. She took it. There were no sounds though, no ringing—at least, not right away. But then there were lots of clicking sounds. Finally, she could hear the phone ring. Her heart began beating hard.

What should she say? What would they say? She looked at Tim, her eyes wide.

She heard a voice on the other end of the line. "Hello?" it said. And then the voice said *hello* two more times before Emma could get any words out.

"Hello!" she said back. She swallowed. "This is Emma," she said. "You know, Emma O'Fallon?"

"Emma! This is Brigid. What's wrong, me darlin'?"

"Nothing," Emma said.

"Nothing?" Brigid said.

"Nothing," Emma said. She could hardly speak for some reason. She felt scared. Or shy. "Nothing's wrong," she said finally.

"But, me dear, are you sure you're all right? It's the middle of the night, it is."

"It's only supper time," Emma said. "I mean, it's seven o'clock."

Brigid laughed. "Not here, it isn't. It's two in the mornin', me dear."

"Oh!" Emma said. "Sorry."

"Emma, are you sure everything's all right?" Brigid asked. "Where's Annie?"

"She's upstairs. But Brigid, we wanted to ask you something, Tim and me. We want you and your sisters to come here."

"Oh, me dear," Brigid said. "We got your

letter and your invitation. Sure, and we'd love to come visit you someday."

"You would? When?"

"We're not sure. But someday."

"Soon, though!" Emma said. "You have to come soon."

"Why?" Brigid asked. "Is something wrong?"

"No, honest!" Emma said. "See, it's just that Annie misses you so much. She talks about you all the time. And she wants you to come and meet us. And we can't go there. So if you came, all of you, it would be so cool, and there's lots of room."

"Oh, me dear, we'd love to come. And someday, we will, I promise. We talked about it at supper tonight, Meagan and me and everybody."

"Then when will you come?" Emma asked.

"Oh, we don't know yet. But we'll plan it, all right?"

"Like next week or something?" Emma said. "We could surprise her. We have lots of bedrooms. You wouldn't all have to be scrunched into two rooms."

Brigid laughed. "No, pet, not next week or next month. When Annie comes here, then we can talk about it. How's that?"

Emma could feel tears springing to her eyes. She swallowed hard. This was their last chance to stop Annie from going and to stop Mom from hiring Mrs. Potts.

"We have to save up our money, pet," Brigid said. She sounded like she was yawning. And then she added, "How about we call in a day or two and talk?"

"Call me, though," Emma said. "Not Annie."

"That I'll do," Brigid said. "We'll plan it. Maybe next summer. Wouldn't that be fine?"

It would not be fine. They could not let Annie go away. They could not let Mrs. Potts take over Annie's job and get Annie sent away for good. Emma swallowed again.

"Emma?" Brigid said. "Are you there, me dear?"

Emma nodded. And then she remembered—sometimes, she forgot that people couldn't see her on the phone. "I'm here," she said. But she couldn't think what else to say.

She looked around her room. It was really big. She had a big double-sized bed. One of the sisters could even sleep with her. She looked at her dolls sitting up on a shelf, and her book *The Secret Garden* alongside them. Her big American Girl doll was tilting to one side, and her bride doll was falling the other way. The bride had lost one shoe. Emma wondered where it was. She wondered if Marmaduke had chewed it up. She wondered if McClain would ever stop slamming things. She wondered what in the world she could say to persuade Brigid.

"Emma, is there something you're not telling me?" Brigid asked, suddenly sounding wide awake. "Is Annie sick or something?"

For one minute, Emma thought of saying yes, yes, Annie was sick. They would definitely come if Annie were sick. But no, she couldn't do that. That wouldn't be right at all. The sisters might be scared half to death, thinking something bad was wrong with Annie. "No," she said. "No, Annie's fine. Really."

She looked at Tim. She signaled him with her eyes. *What should I say? They can't come!*

Tim put out his hands, helpless looking.

"Emma," Brigid said. "Are you sure? Is something happening?"

Emma looked around her room again, feeling so sad she had to fight back tears. She looked up at her shelf again—and then she had a thought. Yes! Suddenly, she had an idea, a splendid idea.

"Yes, something's happening," she said. The whole idea began unrolling, right inside her head. She hadn't even planned it—it was just coming to her.

"See, Annie didn't want to tell you," she said. "She didn't want to tell you because she knew you'd come and she didn't want you to have to spend all that money. So that's why I'm calling you instead. To surprise her. Because see, see, something is happening."

Tim started to frown. "What?" he whispered. "What?"

Emma just shook her head. She could hardly believe what she was going to say. She didn't even know where the idea had come from. Well, maybe she did. Maybe it was the dolls. Anyway, it didn't matter. The idea had come. And it was brilliant.

"See," she said. "Annie wants you here. Because . . . because . . . she's getting married!"

And before Brigid could say a word, Emma pushed the off button, and suddenly Brigid and Ireland were very far away.

Chapter Eleven

Annie to the Rescue

The next day was Saturday, and all morning, Emma felt like she'd either burst or jump right out of her skin. Brigid and the sisters really might come. But then again, they might not come. Brigid had said she'd call back in a day or two—call Emma—yet by noon, she hadn't called. Maybe she was sleeping late, since Emma had wakened her in the night. Meanwhile, Annie was packing for Ireland. Even though it was Saturday and her day off, she had invited the kids up to her apartment to help her. It was so confusing. One minute, Emma felt happy and excited. And the next minute, she was worried sick.

What if the sisters called to ask Annie if it were true? Emma didn't think they'd do that, not if they believed it was a surprise. But they might. Also, they might feel kind of bad that Annie hadn't told them such big news. Not only that, but what if they did come and got here and there was no wedding? Emma didn't see how she could find someone for Annie to marry that fast. At Emma's soccer games, she noticed that lots of the big guys hung around Annie and Woof. Sometimes, they pretended they just wanted to play with Woof. But Emma knew that was an excuse to be near Annie. But Annie didn't act like she wanted a boyfriend. She was nice to them, like she was to everyone.

Emma sighed. There were so many things to worry about. And, of course, one of the biggest—what would Mom say when seven sisters descended on them?

Besides her own worries that morning, the whole house was in a grumpy kind of uproar. McClain was in a mean mood. She kept insisting that they had to go get Kelley from Dr. Pete right this minute before someone adopted her. She made Annie call Dr. Pete every single hour to be sure Kelley was still there. It didn't seem to matter to her at all that Mom had said no cat in the house.

Ira and Lizzie got into a mess. It was drizzly,

and Daddy let them go out in the yard with him while he repaired the back step. They were supposed to be on the swings, but instead, they decided it would be great fun to make mud pies under the swing set. When Daddy finally brought them back in, they were so covered in mud, they looked like two fat baby pigs. Mom seemed annoyed, not just at them, but at Daddy. Tim seemed worried, and quiet, too. Emma knew why.

Then, to make everything just awfully, awfully worse, Emma's soccer game was canceled because of the rain. Even though the sun was supposed to come out later, the coaches decided the field would be too wet. Emma hated that, because when Daddy was home, he came to her games with her. With him traveling so much, she didn't get to have alone time with him that much. It was a very, very rotten Saturday morning.

At noon, the sun came out. Annie came downstairs with big, big lollipops for each kid. And although it was her day off, she said she wanted to take the kids for an outing.

"I talked to Dr. Pete on the phone this morning," Annie told Mom. "He said he's got a deer and two sheep in the pen out back. I thought the children would like to see them."

"Yippee!" McClain yelled.

Dr. Pete rescued all sorts of wild creatures. He kept them in a little pen behind his office till they got better and could go back into the woods. Or if they couldn't go back to the wild, someone would usually adopt them. People were allowed to come visit the animals, but there were rules—you had to be quiet and not scare them. And you couldn't feed them. That's because Dr. Pete said he had special diets for each one.

Ira grabbed Annie's legs. "A sheep?" he said. "I love sheeps."

"That would be nice, Annie," Mom said. "I think the children need an outing." She looked at McClain. "I don't want to hear one word about that cat, though, you hear?"

McClain scowled.

"Promise?" Mom asked. "Otherwise, you can't go."

McClain scowled some more. Finally, though, she said, "Promise." But she didn't sound too happy about it.

Emma and Mom helped Annie bundle up the little kids in their sweaters and coats. Ira found his shoes all by himself. Tim said he didn't want to go. He wanted to stay with Daddy and learn how to load music in his iPod.

In the car, there wasn't a single grumpy face. McClain forgot about sulking and stamping. Annie started singing "The Wheels on the Bus," and the little kids joined in, and Ira kept pretending that he was tooting the horn.

Even Emma felt happy.

"We'll see Kelley, right?" McClain asked as they turned up the long, gravel drive to Dr. Pete's place.

"Yes, sure we can," Annie said.

"And bring her home?"

Annie laughed. "You heard your mum."

"But someday we'll get her, right?" McClain said.

Annie smiled. "We'll work on that, won't we?" she said.

When they pulled up and stopped, the three little kids tumbled out of the car and raced across the field to the pen. Emma got out more slowly and walked close beside Annie. She wondered if she should tell her about her worries.

As they walked, Emma looked up at Annie. She thought she was the prettiest person she had ever seen. She had the coolest clothes, too. Right now she was wearing jeans, but over them she had on a black lace skirt that came almost to her knees, high-top pink sneakers (Annie called them "trainers"), and a black denim jacket. Emma thought no one in the world but Annie would think to wear a skirt over jeans. And no one in the world would look so cool in it.

She wondered if Annie really would get married someday.

"Annie?" Emma asked, suddenly feeling a little shy. "Do you have a boyfriend?"

Annie looked down at her. "Oh, me goodness, no," she said.

"Why not?" Emma asked. "You're so pretty."

Annie laughed. "Pretty is as pretty does. There's plenty of time for that someday. But not for a long while yet."

That made Emma feel better. Except for what she'd told Brigid.

When they got up to the pen, Annie unlatched the gate, and they all went inside the enclosure. Inside were two brown bunnies in a cage, a deer, two sheep, and a raccoon. Emma walked toward the little deer. He was young, a tiny spotted fawn, and Emma thought he looked sad. One of his front legs was bandaged from his hoof to his knee. She wondered if he felt bad being cooped up in a pen when all his friends were out in the woods. She wondered how he had gotten hurt.

The twins talked to the bunnies while McClain put her arms around one of the sheep. She hugged him, then let go, and hugged the other sheep. She wrapped her arms tight around him and buried her face in his wool. The sheep began to move, trotting slowly away.

"Not too tight, McClain!" Annie called to her. "Stop now. He wants to get away."

"I can't!" she yelled. "I'm stuck!"

Just then, the sheep gave a big shrug or a shudder, shaking McClain off. He loped away across the pen. McClain's lollipop was stuck to his side.

"Give it back!" McClain shouted.

"I'll get it," Emma said. She ran to where the sheep had stopped. Carefully, she peeled the lollipop off him. It came away, but it was very, very fuzzy. She carried it back to McClain.

McClain made a face at it, but she licked it anyway. "Yuck!" she said.

"Oh, me word," Annie said, shaking her head. "Why not give me that? Let's throw it away and go inside and see Kelley now."

Only, they didn't have to go inside. At that moment, Dr. Pete came walking across the grassy lawn, a little gray ball of fur in his arms.

"Kelley!" McClain yelled. She ran out of the pen toward Dr. Pete. She moved so fast, she ran right into him and almost knocked him over. "Whoa!" he said, backing up a little. "You little bulldozer, you. Sit down, and you can hold her. But don't let go of her. We don't want her to run off into the woods."

McClain sat down on the ground, and Dr. Pete bent over and carefully placed Kelley in McClain's arms.

"Oh, Kelley!" McClain said. "You've gotten fat! Look, Emma, look how fat she got."

Well, in just one day, she wasn't exactly fatter. But she did look better somehow. Emma was happy about that. She thought how good it was that they had rescued her from starving. Ira and Lizzie came and patted Kelley, too, all of them telling her how fat and cute she was. After a while, the twins got tired of Kelley and went back to playing with the sheep. Emma sat with McClain for a long while, petting Kelley, while Dr. Pete talked to Annie and visited with the animals inside the pen.

Soon, though, the sky got dark, and big fat

raindrops began falling again.

"I think Kelley should get in out of the rain," Dr. Pete said, coming toward them. "What do you think, McClain? Cats don't like rain much." He held out his arms for Kelley.

McClain stood up. Her face was all scrunched up and sad looking. But, obediently, she held Kelley out to Dr. Pete. She kissed Kelley's nose. "Here, Dr. Pete," she said sadly. "Here's your cat."

She looked so sad that for a minute, Emma felt kind of mad at Annie. She knew it was silly of her. But it seemed mean to let McClain come back and see the cat and then have to leave it.

"She's not my cat," Dr. Pete said, taking Kelley and ruffling up her fur. "She's Annie's cat. I'm just boarding her till Annie gets back from her trip."

McClain frowned. "Annie's cat?"

"Oops!" Annie said. "I wasn't going to tell yet."

"Tell what?" McClain said.

"Well, see," Annie said slowly, looking from McClain to Emma and then back. "See, your mum said *you* couldn't have a cat."

"I know. I can't," McClain said.

"Right," Annie said, smiling a little. "But she

didn't say *I* couldn't have a cat. But you mustn't tell. Not yet!"

Emma started to smile. She knew exactly what was happening. McClain didn't understand it yet, but she would in a minute. Annie had adopted Kelley. Kelley would go home with them and live in their house. Only she'd live upstairs in Annie's part of the house. For the first time in a long time, Emma felt really happy inside.

She thought Annie was probably the best person in the whole entire world.

Chapter Twelve

A Call from Ireland

Now, if only Mom and Daddy would think so, too. When Emma got home from Dr. Pete's that day, Tim raced down the stairs to meet her.

"Come to my room," he said. "Come on. Quick!" He turned and ran back up the steps, Emma following him. When they got to his room, they went inside, and he closed the door. He turned to her. "Somebody called," he said.

"Somebody who?"

"Brigid, maybe. I think."

"How do you know? Did you talk to her?"

Tim shook his head. "No, but she must have asked for you, because I heard Mom say Emma isn't home, and then they talked awhile, and then Mom got this funny look on her face, and then she took the phone into her office. I think she's still talking."

"Uh oh," Emma said.

"Daddy talked on the phone, too, for a minute."

"Should we listen?" There was a place in the hall where you could hear everything going on in Mom's office if you stood in just the right place.

Tim shook his head. "I tried," he said.

"What'd you hear?"

"Nothing. Something about plane tickets. That's all."

"Oh!" Emma said. "Maybe they were asking Daddy to help them get tickets because he works for the airline. I bet!"

"But Emma," Tim said. "What if they come and they expect a wedding and there isn't one?"

Emma sighed. She shrugged. "I don't know. Maybe they won't mind. I mean, the biggest thing is they get to see Annie, right? They might even be relieved. I mean, maybe they don't want Annie to be married. Annie said today that she doesn't want to get married yet and—"

"Yes!" Tim interrupted. "But suppose Mom and Daddy now think she *is* getting married? They might decide she shouldn't work for us anymore, at least, she couldn't live upstairs if she's married and—"

"Oh," Emma said. "Ohmigosh, yeah. I didn't think of that." And then she thought and whispered, "Kelley."

"Kelley?" Tim asked.

Emma just shook her head. She couldn't tell Tim about it, not right then. It felt as if her head were swimming, and her heart was doing that funny thing inside her that it did sometimes, acting like it was hammering its way out of her insides.

"Emma!" It was Daddy calling from the hall below. "Emma, come down here, please. We want to see you in Mom's office."

Uh oh. Emma looked at Tim.

"I'll go with you," Tim said.

"Thanks," she said.

They both went down the stairs. As they passed the playroom, they saw Daddy putting a video in for the little kids. He looked up at them. "I'll be there in a minute," he said. "And Tim, we don't need you."

"I want to come," Tim said.

They both went along the hall to Mom's office. Mom was sitting in the big chair behind her desk.

To Emma's surprise, Annie was there, too, standing by the front window, her back to them. She turned when they came in. And she looked mad, plenty mad. Emma didn't think she had ever seen Annie look angry.

Emma couldn't help it. Tears sprang to her eyes. She didn't blame Annie for being mad at her. It was dumb what she had done. And she bet anything the sisters were mad and Mom and Daddy were mad and everything.

She and Tim went and sat down on the little sofa, side by side. In a minute, Daddy came in, too, and he sat in a chair across from Mom's desk.

They all looked at one another.

"I don't think we need you here, Tim," Mom said.

"Oh, I think we do," Annie said.

Emma looked up, surprised. Annie was mad at Tim, too? Or—it seemed weird, but it was almost as though Annie was mad at Mom? Or was it Daddy?

Mom frowned at Annie. "All right," she said slowly. "Why don't you sit down, Annie?"

"I feel fine right here," Annie said.

"All right," Mom said.

She turned to Emma. "Emma, what's going on? We got a phone call from Annie's sister Brigid. Brigid said you called her. She said you told her Annie was getting married. And she said you invited her and the other girls to come visit. Is that true?"

Emma nodded miserably.

Mom turned to Annie. "Annie, are you getting married?" she asked.

"Would I not have told you?" Annie said quietly.

Mom looked a little embarrassed. "Of course you would," she said.

Mom turned back to Emma. "Emma? Why did you call Brigid and say Annie was getting married if she isn't?"

"I called, too," Tim said. "We did it together. It wasn't just Emma."

Both Mom and Daddy looked surprised. Annie raised her eyebrows. She smiled at them slightly.

The smile gave Emma a little courage.

"And why did you do that?" Daddy asked.

"Because," Emma said, "because I wanted to get her sisters to come here. So Annie wouldn't leave us. I asked them, but Brigid said no, not yet, they had to save up, and then I thought that if there was a good reason, they would come, but I couldn't think up a good reason, like I couldn't say Annie was sick, because that wouldn't be nice, but then I saw my bride doll on my shelf, and it just popped into my head, because . . . because it did."

"Because why?" Mom said.

"Because they didn't want me to leave," Annie said softly.

"That's nonsense," Daddy said.

"No, it's not nonsense," Annie said, still in that soft voice. "Not if you're a little kid, it's not. Not if they think I might not come back to them."

"But you are coming back!" Mom said. "Aren't you?"

Annie smiled. "Yes, I am," she said. She turned and looked out the window. "Unless maybe you hire someone else instead," she added. She didn't turn back from the window when she said that.

"Well, whatever gave you that idea?" Mom said. "We'd never do that!"

"Really!" Daddy said. "I don't understand you, Annie. Where'd you get that from?"

"Because you do it all the time, that's why," Emma said.

"We do not!" Mom said.

"You do too," Tim said.

"You do. That's why I called Brigid," Emma said. "'Cause if Annie goes, she might not come back. You'll hire somebody else, like Mrs.

Potts or something. I can tell you like her. You always do that."

"Do not!" Mom said. She looked at Daddy. And then she asked, kind of quietly, "Do we?"

"Well, maybe. I guess," Daddy said slowly. "Kind of." But then he added, "Annie's family! That's different. You don't get rid of family!"

Emma looked at Tim. He moved closer to her.

"Right!" Mom said. She turned to Annie. "You're not thinking of leaving us, are you?"

For a long minute, Annie didn't answer. Then she turned back from the window. She crossed the room to the sofa where Tim and Emma sat. She nudged her way into the middle, between them. She put an arm around each of them, pulling them close.

"No, I'm not thinking of leaving them," she said. "Since I'm family. Maybe when they're all grown up and getting married themselves, I might."

Everyone in the room seemed to breathe better.

"Annie," Daddy said. "We thought you understood that—well, that you're part of the family."

"The children understood," Annie said quietly.

Emma grinned and took a deep breath. She leaned against Annie, and Tim leaned against her from the other side.

Suddenly, they all seemed to notice something at the same time. Ira and Lizzie and McClain were standing in the doorway. Usually they arrived like a herd of elephants. This time, though, they must have come tiptoeing. They stood very close to one another, looking a little scared.

"Is the video over?" Daddy asked.

They didn't answer. All three of them looked from Daddy to Mom, and then to Annie and Tim and Emma on the sofa. They came scurrying across the room. They climbed up onto the sofa, clambering over Annie and Emma and Tim, pushing their way in to make room for themselves.

They all snuggled together.

Annie looked down at them. "I'm not leaving," she said quietly. "Except for three weeks to see me sisters in Ireland. And then I'll be back."

"What about Mrs. Potts?" Emma asked. "Is she going to take care of us while you're gone?"

Annie looked at Mom and Daddy. Mom had come around from behind her desk. Daddy had gotten out of his chair. The two of them stood side by side in front of the desk. They stood very close together. For a minute, Emma thought they looked a little like she and Tim did when they were in trouble, standing real close to each other.

"Well, I've changed my mind about Mrs. Potts," Annie said. "I don't think she's a good choice to care for the children."

"Who will take care of us then?" McClain asked. "I mean, till you come back." And she added, in a whisper, "With Kelley?"

Emma squeezed McClain's leg. "Hush!" she whispered.

"Oh," McClain said softly.

Annie didn't answer. Nobody answered. Neither Mom nor Daddy seemed to have noticed what McClain had said about Kelley.

McClain asked again. "Who will take care of us? Till Annie comes back."

Emma squeezed her leg again, so she wouldn't add "with Kelley."

"I think," Mom said after a minute, "I do think we can do it pretty well ourselves." She looked at Daddy. She looked a little worried. "Do you?"

Daddy nodded. "Yes," he said. But he looked worried, too. "Maybe my mom could come. She hasn't been here since last Christmas."

"Grandma Libby?" Tim and Emma cried together. All the kids really liked Grandma Libby. Grandma Libby was cool. She was so cool, they didn't even call her Grandma half the time. She liked to be called Countess.

"If she'd come, that would be great!" Mom said. "It would be a big help."

"She'll come," Daddy said. "I'm sure of it. I'll call her tonight. She'll be glad to help."

"Tell her not to worry," Emma said. "I'll help, too."

Chapter Thirteen

Annie Goes Away

The day had come. Annie was leaving. The car that was to take her to the airport was waiting at the curb. The school bus for the kids would be along any minute, and Grandma Libby would arrive before the kids got home from school.

Emma and Tim had their lunches and their backpacks all ready, out front on the steps. Emma had the soccer book in her backpack, the stolen book. When Emma had finally gotten Annie alone, she had confessed about the stolen book—the one Marmaduke had chewed up into little shreds. Together, Annie and Emma decided that Emma just had to tell the truth. Annie had ordered the book online, and it had come yesterday.

Emma didn't know which was worse—Annie leaving or taking the book to school.

Mom and Daddy had given Annie some going-away presents. They gave her three of those disposable cameras so she could take lots of pictures. They gave her cookies and fruit to take on the plane and a pretty new red sweater and little presents to give to her sisters. Emma and all the kids had made presents for the sisters, too. The little kids had made plaques with their handprints, Tim had written them a story, and Emma had written a letter. She decorated it with sticker stars so that it was super pretty. She also added a little note about Annie not getting married—that it was all a big mistake, Emma's mistake. But she wrote that she still hoped they would come visit soon—maybe next summer.

Daddy took Annie's bags to the car. They all stood looking at one another. Then Annie turned to the kids. She took each one in her arms. She gave each a kiss. She gave them huge hugs. She promised she'd be back. With presents. She reminded them that they had the paper chain they had made; they could tear off one link for each day she was gone. When there were no links left, she'd be back that day.

The last person she hugged was Emma.

"It's okay if you go," Emma said.

"I know," Annie answered. She pulled Emma close. "You okay?" she whispered quietly. "I mean, about the book?"

Emma nodded. "I'm scared," she said.

"But you can be brave, right?" Annie said.

Again, Emma nodded. "I'll have to admit I told a lie," she said.

Annie nodded. "That will be hard!" she said. "But you'll feel better afterward."

"Promise?" Emma said.

Annie laughed. "Promise," she said.

She turned and went down the steps and got in the car. The kids lined up on the steps, standing close to Mom and Daddy.

"Bye, Annie!" Ira yelled. "'Member my helmet."

"Bye, Annie!" Lizzie yelled. "'Member my Pretty Ponies."

"Take care, Annie!" Mom called.

"Have fun!" Daddy said. "Don't forget to take pictures."

"Bye-bye, Annie," McClain yelled. "Come home soon."

"Bye, Annie," Tim shouted.

Only Emma didn't say anything. She just

waved. She kept on waving till the car turned the corner and disappeared.

Chapter Fourteen

All Better

The only thing good was that this was Wednesday, the day Mrs. Adams had the class meeting. Emma would ask to go first. She would tell the truth, and she wouldn't stop telling till she had said the whole thing. She hoped like anything that she wouldn't throw up, or even worse, cry. Although, every time she thought about it, her knees got wobbly, and her heart started pounding, and she really did feel like she'd throw up. She had gone over and over in her head what she would say. But each time she did, she got scared, and the right words wouldn't come. Annie had said she shouldn't think about what to say, that the right words would jump into her head when it was time.

Emma wasn't so sure of that. How could there be "right words" when what she had done was so wrong?

At school, at the class meeting, all the kids pulled their chairs into a circle with Mrs. Adams. Emma brought the book with her. It was still in its wrapping from Amazon.com, and she put it on the floor under her chair. It was a very flat little package, and when Luisa asked what it was, Emma shook her head. "Later," she whispered. "I'll tell you later."

Already her heart was thundering, and her cheeks were burning. Before Mrs. Adams could even speak, she raised her hand. "Mrs. Adams?" she said. "Can I go first?"

"In a minute, Emma," Mrs. Adams said. "After some announcements. I need to talk about good citizenship awards that will be given out soon, maybe next week, and—"

"But Mrs. Adams!" Emma said. "You can't! Not yet! Please?"

"Emma, you know that announcements come first."

"I know, but this is important!" Emma said. "It's super important. It—it matters!"

She looked over at Jordan. He seemed forlorn. Emma didn't know if he'd been good or not so good. But she knew Mrs. Adams kind of blamed him for the missing book. She'd think better of him after Emma told the truth. Maybe even next week he could get the good citizenship award for most improved.

Mrs. Adams frowned. "All right, Emma," she said slowly. "Since it seems so vital to you. Go ahead. We'll see whether it's really urgent."

Emma took a deep breath. She clenched her hands into little fists. She held them tight in her lap and looked down at them. "Okay," she said. "You know . . . ? I mean . . . you know about the soccer book? I mean, you know about Katie's book? And you know how it disappeared and Katie thought, I mean, she still thinks Jordan stole it? I mean, took it?"

She paused but didn't look up. It was very quiet in the room. Nobody was wiggling or moving their chairs around or anything.

"But he didn't steal it. I did. I mean, I didn't actually *steal* it. I just thought I'd borrow it overnight. But then Marmaduke, you know, that's my ferret, I brought him to school once to show you? Well, he ate up the book while I was asleep. It was like practically gone, nothing left but teeny little pieces."

Emma paused to take another breath. She

still didn't look up. She didn't know if people were staring at her or laughing or what. She didn't care—not too much, anyway. She reached under her chair. She picked up the package.

"I'm sorry," she said. "I know I shouldn't have borrowed it. And I hate that Jordan was getting blamed for it. But I ordered a new one, and it just came, and here it is, and that's all."

She looked up as she held out the package to Katie. Katie just stared at her. The whole class stared at her. Mrs. Adams stared at her, too.

Finally, Katie reached for the book. She still didn't say anything. Nobody said anything. And then Jordan spoke up.

"That is way cool," he said quietly. "Emma is way cool."

"Wonderful!" Mrs. Adams said, smiling. "Emma, thank you. It must have been very hard to do what you just did. And I think that shows what good citizenship is all about. I appreciate it. I think we all do." She looked around the circle. "Don't we, class?"

All the kids nodded. A couple of them clapped. Even Katie was smiling and nodding.

Emma swallowed hard. She couldn't speak. She just looked down in her lap again. She felt so relieved. She sucked in a deep breath. Her heart had stopped thudding so furiously.

"Well," said Mrs. Adams. "I think we can move on now."

The class meeting went on, and the other kids talked about friends and homework and citizenship and all. As they discussed things, Emma thought about what had happened. She was so happy for what Jordan said. She was so happy that Mrs. Adams wasn't mad. Maybe she was brave and maybe she wasn't. But one thing she knew was true. Annie was definitely right: she *did* feel better.

Emma felt better and better all through the day, and when Jordan stole her hat on the playground and played keep-away with it, she laughed, because she knew he was only playing. Maybe it was his way of saying thanks. Emma kept right on feeling good. And when she and Tim got off the school bus at the end of the day, and Annie wasn't there, she felt a little pain in her heart. But when she found Grandma Libby in the playroom, along with Daddy and the little kids, she knew it was going to be all right. Just three more weeks. And Annie would be home again.

Now it was time for Mallomars.